#1 BEST SELLING AUTHOR OF TY HARD

LAURA HARNER

WILLOW SPRINGS RANCH BOOK 4

HANGINGCHAD

Hanging Chad
Willow Springs Ranch #4
Laura Harner

Copyright

Hanging Chad is a work of fiction. Names, characters, places, and incidents are the product of the author's imagination or are used fictitiously. Any resemblance to actual persons, living or dead, events, or locales is entirely coincidental.

Copyright © 2013 by Laura Harner
Cover photograph by DWS Photography
Cover Art by Laura E. Harner
Edited by Jae Ashley
All rights reserved.
ISBN: 978-1-937252-62-5
Published by Hot Corner Press.

Warning: All rights reserved. No part of this book may be reproduced in any many without written permission, except for brief quotations embodied in critical articles and reviews.

The unauthorized reproduction or distribution of this copyrighted work is illegal. Criminal copyright infringement, including infringement without monetary gain is investigated by the FBI and is punishable by up to five years in federal prison and a fine of $250,000. eBooks are not transferable. They cannot be sold, shared or given away as it is an infringement on the copyright of this book.

Contact the publisher for further information: Hotcornerpress@gmail.com

Dedication

For the fans of the Willow Springs Ranch series. Your support means more than you will ever know.

Tom Webb, Jae Ashley, Dan Skinner, Lee Brazil, and Havan Fellows—your contributions are greatly appreciated.

Finally, a special thank you to Will Parkinson—for everything!

I would also like to acknowledge the men and women of the Arizona Department of Economic Services and Child Protective Services. You perform an incredibly difficult service. Any errors in the agency's processes or policies portrayed in this work of fiction are mine.

Acknowledgement of Trademarks

The author acknowledges the trademarked status and trademark owners of the following trademarks mentioned in this work of fiction:

Boy Scout: Boy Scouts of America Corporation
Marlboro: Philip Morris USA Inc.
Polaroid: Polaroid Corporation
Twinkies: Hostess Brands, Inc.
Crocs: Crocs, Inc.
Starbucks: Starbucks Corporation
VW: Volkswagen Aktiengesellschaft
Corporation

Table of Contents

Chapter One

Eight seconds. Eight bone-jarring, teeth-rattling, mind-numbing seconds. He focused on form and forced his body to ignore everything except matching the rhythm of the big bronc. Keep it smooth. Spurs to the tip of the shoulders. Hand raised. Heels to the saddle. Tighten that grip. Focus. Don't count. Just go. Just go. *Buzz.*

"Come on, cowboy. Good ride." The hand reaching for him was a lifeline, there to pull him from the back of meanest bronc of the weekend. Before he could feel the first stirrings of satisfaction for sticking the ride, all hell broke loose. Black Fury seemed to take a personal offense to the buzzer or the announcer's voice over the loud speaker. With a mighty thrust of his haunches, he re-doubled his efforts to be free—not only of Jesse—but also free from the two pick-up riders and their horses.

Thousands of pounds of horseflesh slammed together with all the force of train wreck. Poised between his saddle and safety, Jesse slipped out of the cowboy's grip and tumbled into the abyss. Mashed against the wooden boards, but lost in the dusty confusion of hooves, haunches, and hands, Jesse couldn't get any purchase to clamber over the fence. Caught in the no-man's land between the side of the ring and tons of pissed-off bronc, Jesse hunched his shoulders and covered his head and neck in an instinctive gesture to stay alive.

When hands touched his shoulder, then his head, he realized it was over and slid down the wall onto the arena floor, too stunned to even know whether or not he was hurt.

"Can you walk, Duran?" Buck's voice was a whisper to avoid carrying in the suddenly silent arena, and both men knew all eyes were on them.

"Yeah. Give me a sec." His voice squeezed painfully out between two flat pieces of cardboard that used to be his lungs.

Riding rough stock, you could expect certain things as regular as the next day's sunrise. First, it was gonna hurt. Even if you stuck, it still hurt. Second, if you fell and it didn't kill you, you better get your ass out of the dust before they brought the stretcher. Because once a cowboy got carted off, he was out of the money for the rest of the rodeo and he had to fight his way back into the next rodeo on the circuit because the damn doctors never understood the concept of *'good enough.'*

No way could Jesse afford to be out of the money that long. He'd run out of the national sponsors years ago and was barely getting the local sponsors now. He'd be damned if he had to start digging too deep into his savings in order to pay for entrance fees.

"Fuck. Okay, let's do this." He let the strong hands of Buck and George help him to his feet. They all made it look easy as Jesse waved his black hat to the now-cheering crowd, and none of them mentioned just how much of his weight the other two men supported.

As soon as they were out of sight of the stands, George maneuvered him to a bench. The two men ran back to their positions near the chute before the next rider mounted and the show went on. Just like it would once Jesse could no longer ride. A time that seemed to be drawing nearer every day. Spotting the rodeo doc heading his way, Jesse stood quickly to prove he was still fit. And promptly doubled over and puked up what was left of his double cheeseburger from lunch. *Lovely.*

"I'm too old for this shit."

"Ya' think?" Doc Cranston looked up at the standings board and pursed his lips. "Only three more riders left…and you have the score to beat. Need me to help you to the tent, Duran?"

"Come on, Doc. I don't have any more rides this weekend. Can't you just sign me off?"

"Nope. Under your own power or mine?" Doc gripped his upper arm and started to pull, but Jesse jerked free.

"I got it." Moving on sheer pride and stupidity, Jesse hobbled the twenty feet to the medical tent, determined to keep his qualified-to-ride status.

Biting back the groan when he climbed onto the exam table, Jesse breathed shallowly through his mouth, hoping like hell he hadn't cracked a rib.

"Okay, you know the drill, cowboy. Shirt off. I'm going to look for anything obvious, then send you over to Colbert General for x-rays. Did he get your legs or just the chest?"

"Just my chest—" Jesse was cut off by a voice from his past.

"Hey, I hear you got an old man in here who thinks he can still keep up with all the young rodeo studs. Mind If I talk to your patient, Doc?"

"Hey, Roy. I'm barely fucking old enough to buy you a drink, so I guess the next round's on you." Jesse gasped the words and pretended the accusation didn't sting. "How the hell are you, anyway, old timer?" He grinned at the ancient cowboy, more glad than he could say to see his old friend from the circuit. Hell, he and Roy went back to Jesse's first rodeo outside the junior circuit—and he'd thought the man had been old then. Of course, everyone over thirty looks old when you're seventeen.

"I'm good. Living here now with my daughter, you know…"

"Here? You and Gibby didn't split—aww fuck. What happened?"

Roy stared back out toward the arena for a few minutes while Doc Cranston pressed against Jesse's sides. Apparently satisfied the ambulance wasn't necessary, the doctor patted his shoulder and moved over to his makeshift desk to write out the order.

Jesse moved slowly to slip his shirt back on and waited for Roy to tell him what happened. Frank Gibson had been Roy's long time partner, and last he'd heard they were getting fat and happy on some ranch down Arizona.

Roy finally nodded. "Yeah, Frank had a heart attack right there on the Willow Springs. It was quick."

"I'm sorry, man."

Roy nodded again, then turned to face him, face serious. "How sorry?"

Jesse blinked. "You need a favor? I can do anything but quick cash. I've got a little saved, but not easy—"

"I don't need your money, son. The owner of the WSR, Cass Cartwright, is a good man. He took good care of me after Frank died—helped me get up here to my daughter's place. Woulda let me stay on at the ranch as long as I wanted."

Jesse slid from the table, only wincing slightly as he limped over to the doctor and held out his hand for the x-ray order.

"Don't think you can duck out of this, Duran. I'm entering it into the database. Without medical clearance, you aren't riding at Steamboat next month. There's a prescription for some pain medication. If it's worse than bruised ribs, the doctors at the hospital will give you something else." Cranston rested a hand on Jesse's shoulder. "You know, Duran, you're old enough to know better. Riding rough stock is a young man's sport. One of these days, and probably sooner rather than later, you're going to break your fucking neck and need a nurse to feed you and wipe your ass. Listen to what Roy has to say."

Jesse whipped his head around to look at the old man, then nearly went over sideways from the pain in his side. *Fuck that hurt.*

"You two are in on this together? Come on, Roy—give it up. What's this so-called favor?"

Two hours later, Jesse drove past Colbert General without stopping for the x-rays. His gaze briefly strayed to the bed of his pickup, to where everything he owned was stored in an old duffle bag and a few boxes. He patted the pocket of his shirt, feeling the reassuring brush of the first-place check. It wasn't much, but it was enough to keep him in gas and food until he got to the next show. Even if that was in west bumfuck Arizona and had nothing to do with the rodeo.

With a pained groan, Jesse leaned forward and pressed the play button on his favorite rodeo playlist. He hummed quietly along with Chris LeDoux and headed south. He had twelve hours to think about his promise to Roy. Maybe he'd tack on a night or two in Laughlin before he headed to the Willow Springs.

****

Eight seconds, Chad. Just like a cowboy. That's not too much. You're eight years old, now, it's time to stop acting like a baby.

The dream was back, mixing grown up observations with childhood fears… Twenty-four-year-old Chad—no, twenty-five as of midnight—stood next to his eight-year-old self. Memories and dreams juxtaposed, as if he hung suspended above a pond of still water just before he splashed away his own reflection. The ripples still moving him in unanticipated directions. What if the next five minutes had never happened…

"I don't want to, Dad. Please don't make me." The low-hanging black clouds and the long low rumble of thunder had been a perfect backdrop for the storm of temper he had tried to hold back.

"Nonsense, Chad. It's your eighth birthday. Get on the goddamn horse this minute!"

"But—"

The blow to the back of his head had been shocking. No one had ever hit him on the head before. It had always been a strap to the butt and never in front of the horses. God knew you didn't want to spook the horses.

Chad had swallowed his words along with the tears that threatened, but it hadn't been enough to stop him from shaking as he held the reins in one hand and reached up for the saddle horn.

For some reason known only to his father, the fear a seven-year-old had for horses was not acceptable once he turned eight. Before he'd gotten his boot fully inserted in the stirrup, his dad hefted him up and Chad landed on the back of the farm's prize American Quarter Horse stud. At seventeen hands, Rajun' was bigger than most, but his offspring were beautiful, and his annual earnings paid for everything else around the farm.

So there he was, on the back of the tallest Quarter Horse in Western New Mexico and Northern Arizona, shivering and biting his lip to keep from begging to get down. The slap to Rajun's rump might has well have been a gunshot. The beast's powerful haunches bunched and he surged forward, racing toward the open paddock gate, heading straight for the foothills. Grown up Chad felt the sting of tears as the fresh pain of the dream dragged him further into the past.

A silent scream split Chad's mouth as he gripped the pommel with both hands. He fought to remain seated as they raced through the gate, along barbed wire fence, faster than wind, and straight toward the black storm clouds obscuring the northern sky.

Further and faster than Chad believed possible. He risked a look over his shoulder, but blowing dust and distance obliterated every familiar landmark. They raced with heart-stopping speed until tears streamed and he sobbed for someone—anyone—to make it stop. In the end, Mother Nature put an end to the ride, but not to his fear or pain. Chad's hair stood on end, the crackle of electricity the only warning before the sky exploded, a white-hot flash that lit up the night, accompanied by the cannon crack of thunder. Rajun' skittered, then reared and Chad flew sideways through the air, landing in a tangle of limbs, fence post, and two-strand…

Enough… the twenty-five-year-old Chad fought his way out of the dream, tangled in sheets, soaked in sweat, heart trying to claw out of his chest. It was over. *Over.*

A quick glance at the blue digital readout confirmed he'd only been sleeping an hour. If he tried to sleep now, the dream would return… That was enough to have him pushing to his feet. He grabbed his jeans and boots. From the closet, he took the only hanging shirt he'd brought along—a fancy aqua button front that Bryan had given him to go along with the birthday weekend in Laughlin that Cass and Ty insisted on.

*

Thirty minutes later, he was showing his ID to the bartender and ignoring the smirk from the cowboy on the next barstool.

While Chad waited for his margarita, he looked around the club. Two in the morning of his twenty-fifth birthday and he was alone in a bar in Laughlin, Nevada. It was enough to make a grown man cry. That fucking dream…memory…whatever. They'd had to cut him out of the two-strand, and after three surgeries, and months of physical therapy, he'd finally learned to walk again. Rajun' hadn't been so lucky. Six months after the accident his father killed himself and his mother sold the farm to pay off their debts.

"You running a tab?" the bartender asked, startling him from the memories and setting down a glass with a bowl big enough to house a family of goldfish.

"I got this one, Chris," the cowboy said, sliding a twenty-dollar bill across the damp wood.

Surprised, Chad turned to look at the man on the next stool. Good looking enough if you believed the whole Marlboro Man costume…which Chad definitely didn't. With the black felt cowboy hat, western shirt with pearl snaps, and tight blue jeans, it was easy enough to tell the dude was a poser. Although the boots looked battered enough to be real—which meant he'd probably bought them secondhand. Well, if there was one certainty in Chad's life it was he didn't do cowboys. Not ever. Because cowboys had horses…

Eight seconds, Chad. He pulled back a shudder as the tendrils of his dream threatened to pull him back, even here.

"Everyone deserves to have someone else pay for his first grown up drink. Let me guess, it's your birthday, right? Where's your parents, kid?"

"Nice…are you always so condescending? I'm twenty-five — so if you want your money back, talk to the bartender. And oh, look. The bimbo with the beehive hair looks to have gotten her costume the same place you did. How nice. Is she with you?" Chad took a sip, ready to keep sparring if necessary.

The man threw his head back and laughed, a deep rich baritone. The movement gave Chad a look at the chiseled features hidden by the wide brim of the hat. He was a good looking man, maybe in his late thirties or early forties, with short dark hair, a thin face with winkles that fanned away from his eyes and deep creases bracketing his mouth as he laughed. The humor looked good on him. Whichever woman this wannabe cowboy targeted tonight would fall pretty quickly to his charms.

The faux cowboy grabbed his long neck bottle and tilted his head back, throat working as he finished his beer. He set the bottle down on the table and grinned at Chad. "Boy's got a bite — "

"Fuck you…"

The man stood, unfolding himself to his full height. Grabbing his crotch, he drew Chad's gaze to the impressive bulge hanging just left of center. "Oh, I doubt you swing my way, youngster, but thanks for the thought." He tipped his hat to the bartender. "Chris. Good to see you again."

"You too, Mr. Duran. Take care."

"Happy birthday, kid." Then on long legs that were just a little bowed, the stranger sauntered from the bar, his slim hips rolling underneath his denim-cased tight ass, and Chad's mouth went a little dry. *Fuck.*

Chad saw enough cowboys at the WSR to choke a horse. He laughed at his own joke and took a sip of his icy green drink. He'd been wrong—the man wasn't a poser—that walk was pure cowboy. Too bad for Chad the man was just another lost opportunity. Because he was sure they swung the same way...but cowboys were off the menu. Period.

Chapter Two

The place had a good set up, Jesse thought as he coasted the last fifty feet before pulling to a stop next to several other trucks parked on one side of a hard-packed dirt yard. He climbed out of the truck and took a few minutes to stretch his back while he surveyed his surroundings, pretending he could walk if he wanted. Truth was, he was still pretty damned beat up, even after taking a couple of days in Laughlin to recuperate. He needed to get back on a horse today—shake things loose.

Across from the long, low ranch house were three small adobe-style homes, each looking uniquely lived-in, from the curtains blowing in the open windows to an assortment of boots on the porches. The thought that one of those must be where Roy and Gibby had lived made him smile—although he'd bet theirs wasn't the one with the barrels of flowers and the bright yellow door. The residences were bracketed by a barn on one side and a couple of buildings that were probably bunkhouses on the other.

No one was in the immediate vicinity, but there were several ranch hands near the barn.

Seemed like a big spread. Of course, from what he'd heard, Cartwright could afford to dabble in anything he wanted—he'd just happened to pick ranching. Was pretty damned good at it too, apparently. Quarter Horses and Angus. Well, it was probably a good thing he didn't have any rough stock. Might just keep Jesse out of trouble for a few weeks.

"Hey there," a deep voice growled at him from the doorway. "You Jesse?"

Turning, Jesse closed the truck door and walked the dusty path up to the shady front porch. "Guilty as charged. Jesse Duran," he said. "And you must be Cass? Roy said you could use a temporary ranch hand." They shook and Cass stepped back to allow Jesse to enter.

Cass laughed. "Did he now? Because Roy told me you needed a place to recuperate from some injuries and rest while you figure out what you want to do next."

Jesse looked at Cass for a long moment, then choked out a laugh from his still painful ribs. "Son of a bitch. What do you think the old cuss is up to?"

"I suspect we both got part of the truth. I can use a good hand with horses. I'm looking to expand and need someone who can work with the cutters. Someone who knows what he's doing. I've seen you on the circuit, you'll do." Cass's grin was infectious.

Jesse liked Cass, liked the easygoing acceptance of Roy's good-hearted scheme. He just wasn't sure he was ready to think about retiring from the rodeo. He'd never lived in one place for more than a few months during the off-season…

A big hand clapped him on the shoulder, effectively knocking him from his reverie. "Don't tie yourself up thinking about it, Jesse. You have time. I understand you've got a few bumps and bruises to get over. Far as I know there's about a week and a half until the rodeo at Canyon Springs. Are you registered there?"

"Nope. I promised Roy and the Doc I'd take a month—wait for Steamboat. It was that or they were going with me to make sure I got the x-rays."

"All right, come on to the office and we'll talk about what you're looking to do while you're here. And now that we know Roy wasn't exactly painting a full picture, if you just want to hang out, say so."

"I'm not exactly the sit-around-the-house type. I'll earn my keep."

"Fair enough." Cass led the way into a comfortable looking study. Two dark wooden desks took up one end of the long room, each with a computer, and an assortment of files, stacks of papers, charts, and lists spread over the work surfaces. Cass headed to the workstation on the right and gestured for Jesse to sit in the visitor chair that served both desks.

"I got some paperwork for you to fill out." Cass grinned. "Yeah, I know—but some things can't be helped. I'll show you around, take you to the bunkhouse…"

Cass thumbed through a stack of papers, squinting and cursing.

"Hey, old man, put on your damned glasses."

Jesse looked back toward where a good-looking, dark haired man wearing a white chef's apron over a pair of jeans leaned in the doorway.

Cass glanced up. "Jesse, the impertinent cook over there is Tyler Hardin."

Jesse stood to shake hands when a squawk from the radio on Cass's desk drew everyone's attention.

"Hey, Cass, you there?"

Cartwright picked up the radio. "Right here. What's wrong, Phil?"

"I'm riding the fence in the north quarter, and I just got to marker two forty-three. The goddamn thing's down again, Cass. There's no doubt it's been cut. I need a truck with more two-strand than I've got with me. We've got cattle on the other side, scattered on the Trust land. Gonna need a couple of men on horses."

"Shit—Okay, we'll be out there quick as we can. Twenty minutes tops for the truck. The cattle will be okay until we get there with the horses. Keep the radio nearby."

*

Five hours later, Jesse slid from the back of the badly misnamed Angel, and gave the big black gelding a pat on his sweaty neck. "Whoever named you had a wicked sense of humor. Come on, you nasty-assed bastard, let's brush you down and get you fed." Despite his words, Jesse was smiling as he worked the horse free from his bit and saddle. He was already in love with the ornery beast.

One of the men climbed over the fence surrounding the paddock and hurried to take the saddle. "Here let me get that for you." He propped it over the wood railing while Jesse led Angel to the trough.

"Thanks. I'm Jesse."

"I know. Jesse Duran. I'm Whit. I'm a fan. I saw you ride in Las Vegas. You made it seven rounds."

"Damn, that was a hundred years ago. Nice to meet you, Whit."

Jesse looked out over the extended grounds, his gaze settling on a man and child walking hand-in-hand from the main house to one of the smaller single homes. Another man stepped from the porch and the boy skipped ahead, running straight into outstretched arms. The first man was likely the boy's father, based on their matching dark skin, but given the hugs and kisses exchanged by the two men, this was a small family. Damn. Black, white, gay with a kid. Wasn't this just a progressive place to be? He gave a snort.

"Not gonna be a problem, is it?" Whit asked. Apparently fandom didn't extend to allowing bigotry. Good to know.

"Hell, no. Just not something I'm used to seeing. I amused myself with thinking how progressive a bunch of cowboys in the middle of fucking nowhere can be. Do you have to be gay to work here?"

"Gay, bisexual, or don't give a shit. Cass runs a good place—and there's no room for stupid. Most of us are here full time, others swing through then move on." Whit used his chin to point toward the family Jesse had been watching. "That right there is Holden and Drew, and their boy, Alex. They're good folk."

"There can't be a school within an hour of here. Does the kid go into Kingman everyday?"

"No, we got a school teacher out here right now. Of course, he's also the construction foreman." Whit turned toward a building set off to one side that was obviously still under construction. Jesse followed his gaze.

Based on the shape of the foundation and existing frame, the building looked long and low, but there was no real way to tell the purpose of the new structure without a closer look at the interior framing. Large piles of lumber sat in some sort of organized chaos and a lone man stood on top of a ladder, still hammering boards into place.

"That's your teacher?" Faded jeans cupped a tight bubble butt. *Nice ass.* Aloud he voiced a different opinion. "Working on the building by himself is one way to make sure he sticks around."

Whit laughed. "Chad's just finishing up anything left over from the day. Everyone works on the place. Cass rotates folks around. That's gonna be like a dorm for handicapped kids. And…yeah, I know what you're thinking, it is a nice ass, but it's off limits."

Jesse turned and gave Whit an appraising look. "He yours?"

"Chad? Nope, but he flies solo around here. He got burned in Flag a while back, but I don't think that's what's wrong."

"What do you mean?"

"I'm not sure, but whatever it is, it's Chad's story — and he ain't telling."

Jesse looked back up at the man standing on the roof. God what was it about him that he loved a challenge? He'd climb any fucking mountain, whether it was the meanest bronc or the I-don't-bottom one night stands… Jesse just needed the fucking contest in order to know he was alive. Thinking about retiring from the circuit was killing him, but so was accepting the increasingly smaller rodeos. Pretty damned soon he'd be sitting on toothless Shetlands, shitting his pants, and telling the other cowboys in the retirement home about the time he made it to Finals. *Fuck*. At least the tight ass would be something to work toward while he was here. He squinted into the setting sun and wondered if the front looked as good as the back.

Whit laughed again as if he'd been reading Jesse's mind. "Go for it. You sure wouldn't be the first one to try. You want me to finish Angel?"

"No, I got him. Fucking horse would hold it against me..." Jesse shuffled back as Angel tried to take a bite out of his ass.

****

Chad stood atop his ladder inspecting and reinforcing the work done on the frame by others, just as he did every evening, keeping safely out of the way while the ranch hands were finishing for the day. Not that they weren't perfectly nice, because most of them were. He ate most meals with these same men, played an occasional evening of poker, even went to town with some of them once in a while. It was really only at the end of the day he avoided them, when they rode in from wherever they'd been working, and did all the cowboy shit.

Late every afternoon the smell of men, sweat, and leather mixed with horse and manure hung over the yard, the eau de cowboy cologne marking everything with the stench of his childhood memories. Wild stories met with laughter as the men tried to outdo each other with tall tales about what they'd done during the workday. Cass stood among the men, going along good-naturedly, even as he managed to glean the necessary information to make up the next day's work assignments.

The whole thing was too fucking testosterone-laden and left no room for Chad to breathe through the memories. Now there was some new cowboy on the ranch, some kind of retiring rodeo star. He could hear bits of excited conversation floating on a wisp of evening breeze as more of the men returned.

As he holstered the hammer in his tool belt and picked up a few stray nails, Chad glanced over his shoulder and confirmed the men were gathered around the old man. In fact, all Chad could see was a dusty black cowboy hat surrounded by Whit, Phil, Juan, and the other cowboys. Well, they could have the old coot. He'd rather eat alone in his own place tonight than have to sit through endless rodeo stories at dinner. He firmly pushed aside the memories of a seven year old boy who'd been by turns fascinated and terrified by the big cowboys around his daddy's barn.

"Dinner's on," Ty shouted from the back of the main house.

Working his way down the ladder, carrying more than he should have been, Chad looked over at the men again, and missed the last rung. His ankle twisted slightly, and instinctively, his arms flailed, his weight shifted, and he came down hard. Dots floated before his eyes as pain shot up his left leg to set his lower back and hip on fire. Suddenly numb fingers dropped the bucket of supplies and they fell to the hard-packed ground with a loud crash. "Fuck."

Whit, Cass, and Juan all turned, starting to move his way, calling out, asking if he was all right.

Through sheer determination, Chad remained standing, waving off the approaching group. "I'm okay, just slipped. You all go ahead to dinner, I've already got something fixed back at the house."

"You sure?" Cass called.

"Yep. I'm good, Cass."

"All right. I was going to talk with you after dinner about the upcoming camp, but it'll wait until morning. See you then."

"See you," Chad agreed. He turned around and stared at the scatter of tools. Not many—he could do this. Holding tight to the ladder with one hand, Chad carefully bent from the knees and grabbed the wire handle of the bucket. Then he straightened with equal care, wiped the sweat from his face, and wondered if he could keep from throwing up from the pain. At least until he got to his casita. Shit. He gingerly put a little weight on his left foot, then sucked in air through his teeth with a hiss.

"Hurts like a sonofabitch, doesn't it?"

Chad nearly dropped the bucket again at the unexpected voice right behind him. "You scared the crap out of me," he said and turned. His mind blanked on a name, but he knew this cowboy from somewhere…

"Here, let me get that for you." The stranger took the bucket handle from Chad's numb fingers. "Want me to take the tool belt, too?"

Blinking up at the man's face, Chad tried to catalog the parts underneath the dust from the trail. He knew they'd been chasing down some loose cattle, but surely there was no way this was the old rodeo star? Chad had pictured someone close to sixty…not someone in his thirties or forties. Dark eyes met his, and a spread of crow's feet fanned away as the man smiled down. The memory clicked into place when he saw the deep creases on either side of the wide smile.

"Hey, I know you." The man had left him feeling a little off balance at the bar in Laughlin. They'd barely brushed up against each other, and even then, Chad had thought he was a poser. Something had tickled at him, though, as if there might have been something important he missed, all because of a childhood memory.

"Yeah? Seen me ride somewhere?" The cowboy reached for Chad's tool belt.

Chad laughed, and suddenly feeling back in control, slapped the man's hand away. "Arrogant, much? I meant I saw you the other night at the bar in Laughlin."

The man squinted, pursed his lips. Then the smile broke out again, and nearly forced an answering grin from Chad. "BB. Birthday boy.

How the hell are you?" His voice was full of warmth and laughter, as if they really were old friends. He reached again for the tool belt, but Chad twisted his hips, maintaining a safe distance, but nearly buckling his knees with another sharp pain.

"Aww, is that how you treat an old friend?"

It was hard to look menacing when you were eight inches shorter than someone, but Chad leveled his best teacher's glare at the big cowboy. "We're not friends, I don't even know who you are—"

"Ouch. You mean my fame doesn't precede me? Well, hell. My name's Jesse Duran and I guess you'll just have to get to know me instead of judging me by my reputation then, huh, BB?"

Chad's back was really starting to spasm, but he couldn't seem to shake the persistent man...*Jesse*. "I'm not BB or Birthday Boy, or any other damn thing. My name's Chad Ollom, and whatever it is you're selling, I don't want any. Just hand me that bucket and head to the main house. Ty sets a great meal, and you're already late."

Chad reached for the bucket, but couldn't hide the wince as he leaned forward.

Jesse steadied him with a firm hand on his arm. "All right, Chad Ollom, nice to meet you. Now, I can say with dead certainty there ain't nobody here who understands hiding pain more than I do. Show me where you live and I'll help you get there. Your secret's safe with me." Without waiting for an answer, Jesse squatted and started tossing the spilled tools, boxes of nails, and the measuring tape back into the bucket. When he was finished, Jesse looked up, his face close to Chad's hips. "Jesus, you're gray. I'm taking the goddamn tool belt, too." Still on his knees in the dirt, the other man unfastened the buckle and dropped the worn leather into the bucket.

"Which bunkhouse?" Jesse asked. As if he knew exactly which side hurt most, he moved to the right, wrapped his big arm around Chad's back and hooked his finger into the belt loop.

"Not bunk—" They took two small steps, and Jesse adjusted his grip to take more of Chad's weight, leaving him feeling ridiculously helpless in the big man's arms. "First casita. Straight ahead."

Neither of them spoke, and the yard was silent except for Chad's heavy breathing and occasional gasps when the knifelike stabbing pierced his lower back and shot down his leg.

Jesse opened the door, paused just inside to set down the bucket of tools, and scanned the room. "Which room is yours?"

"Right. But you don't need to—"

Clearly not very good with subtle hints, Jesse continued moving until he got into Chad's bedroom.

"Okay. You got a roommate? Boyfriend?"

"What? No! Look, you can go now. Thanks for the help." Chad made to step away and his left leg buckled. The only thing that kept him from falling was Jesse's arm around his waist.

"Right. Don't get your tight little ass in an uproar. You're going to get undressed," Jesse said, his hands already sliding Chad's T-shirt over his head. "Then I'm gonna put you in the hottest shower you can stand..." Jesse paused while he unfastened Chad's jeans and pushed them around his ankles. Instead of waiting for Chad to step out of the pooled denim, Jesse lifted, and turned them both toward the bathroom. "Let's go."

Then, in the most bizarre shower scene since Psycho, Chad found himself propped chest against the wall, while the big cowboy aimed the hot spray on his back and pushed the heel of his hand against the muscles at the base of Chad's spine.

Thirty minutes later, Chad was face down on his own bed, a pillow under his hips and a bag of frozen peas on the spot where his left hip and lower back met. He could hear Jesse moving around his casita, but couldn't stir the energy to kick him out. Besides, the man had known more than a thing or two about muscle spasms and pain relief.

"Feel like you can take these laying down, or would you rather sit?"

Chad opened his eyes to see two of the horse-sized pain relief pills his doctor prescribed for the occasional flare-up. He reached out and tossed them to the back of his throat, then sipped water through the straw in the glass Jesse had brought.

"Thanks. You didn't have to— Uhm, it's getting kind of late. Where are you staying?" Chad tried to make eye contact, but Jesse pressed his hand onto the frozen veggies, making him hiss with the increased chill.

"I figured your couch would be good. I've got my sleeping bag in the back of my truck."

"No, that's not an option. I don't even know you." Chad tried to sound stern, but there might have been a bit of breathless in his reply. Maybe Jesse would think it was the pain.

"That's why I'm not climbing in bed right along side you, BB. "

"Told you, I'm not Birthday Boy..."

"Oh, hell, I changed that nickname right about the time I dropped your drawers. BB. Beautiful Butt." A calloused hand slid once over the curve of his ass. Then Jesse stood with a deep groan that Chad felt low in his belly.

"Think I'll go get that sleeping bag and stretch out. You just holler if you need help with anything." Jesse removed the makeshift icepack, then stood looking down at him for a long minute. "I'm pretty sure you owe me a good night kiss. I did buy you a drink the other night, after all."

"In your dreams, cowboy."

"Well, you know that's right, blondie." Then Jesse leaned down and pressed their lips together. When his lips parted slightly, Jesse licked at the seam, touched briefly against Chad's tongue, then he pulled back and swiped his thumb over Chad's damp mouth. "Sleep well."

Well shit…

Chapter Three

"Tanner? Are you listening to me? You aren't fucking trying hard enough to disrupt things out there."

Tanner looked up and met eyes too much like his own to deny. "Yes, Dad. I'm listening. I don't know what else you want me to do. I've taken down the fence on the furthest corner of the WSR twice. Last night, I chased a shitload of their new stock out into the brush. It cost them entire day of work for their hands. And like you always say, on a ranch time equals money."

"It ain't enough. I need you to work in close, make it hurt in a big way."

Tanner met his father's gaze, but was fully aware of his brother T-bone standing in the doorway. The little prick wasn't going help dissuade their father from this stupid idea. In fact, he wouldn't be surprised if the whole thing was his idea. Jesus—they were gonna lose everything if this kept up. The Trip-T was his granddad's legacy, divided three ways between him and his brothers, but with his father having a lifetime interest. It broke Tanner's heart to think of letting go.

"Dad, the Willow Springs is way the fuck west of us. They don't even touch our boundaries except for a couple grazing permits on federal land. Why do you care what the hell they're up to? Seems like we have better things to focus on, like more of those bunkers you want built."

"You listen here. What they do out there is an abomination to the Lord. And now they plan to bring children to stay with them. Poor sick children who won't be able to fight back when they are sodomized. We can't let that happen. How can we expect the general will want to continue building his nation here when such venal, unholy acts occur on our doorstep?"

"Jesus Christ, Dad. They're gay, not pedophiles."

"Don't you dare blaspheme in their defense. The WSR is exactly where the pedophile teacher went after he lost his job for molesting that little boy. Now Cartwright is bringing in more children. You do the math. Your brother Thomas is working on getting the teacher brought back to Flagstaff so he can be arrested and properly punished. Your job is to get Cass and his fag partner to sell the ranch."

Tanner blinked at his dad, taking in the hard lines of his weathered face, the nostrils white and flaring with each rapid breath, his mouth an angry slash. He wondered at the hatred spewing from the old man's mouth. *Did he know?*

"I want them gone, and as my eldest son, I expect you to follow my orders. You go back tonight and burn down one of the bunkhouses. We'll take them one at a time until Cartwright has no choice but to sell."

Not acknowledging the order, Tanner stood and moved to the doorway, and faked a yawn, but not the weariness that ran bone-deep. "It was a long night, I'm going to catch a little shut eye. See you both at dinner."

T-bone trailed after him until the got to the hallway. "You aren't going to talk him out of it, you know."

Tanner looked at his brother, saw the narrow mouth curl up on one side, in an imitation of a smile. "The general wants the fags gone on principle, but he wants the WSR for himself. By the time we tie up that land and the Cardwell place, all the land west of here and south of I-40 will belong to us. Believe me, that fuck up with the burro roundup was a blessing in disguise. The new plans are going to give us the independence from the so-called federal government. Once and for all."

Tanner drew himself up, using his extra six inches to stand tall over his younger brother. "I know you, Tim. I know you better than anyone. Whatever bullshit you're feeding Dad or the general, won't work on me. Cass Cartwright will never sell the WSR. We can burn down the whole fucking place, and he's only gonna dig down deeper. Ever since he brought on Sheriff Titus to do that background business, there's a lot of ranchers out here respect the hell out of him and if it ever comes down to a battle between the WSR and the Trip-T...well, I think we might be on the wrong end of that fight."

T-bone leaned in, his voice a whisper that seemed to hold something dark and nasty, like the quiet slither of a snake in the attic. "I know you too, big brother. Your secrets aren't nearly as buried as you think they are... You better back the fuck off, or maybe I'll tell Dad how you always seem to disappear when we go to Laughlin. Maybe I'll follow you next time...or maybe I already know." His smile was a smirk by any standards, but Tanner knew a bullshit fishing expedition when he saw one

"Think what you want, T—I don't give a shit. We both know Dad is sick, and feeding into his paranoia is only making things worse. I'll do what needs to be done, but I suggest you keep the fuck out of my way." Tanner turned on his heel and stalked down the hall. As he reached his room he paused, looked down at his empty hand, and realized he'd forgotten his cell phone. *Shit.* No way was he willing to leave it for his brother to thumb through his contacts. He retraced his steps, but his father's angry words sent a shiver skittering along his spine.

"Timothy, son, I think you're the only one who truly understands the importance of what the general is trying to do out here. This is our place to make a stand, and by God, my family will not be cause for trouble."

"Whatever you need done...you can count on me, Dad."

There was a long pause, and for a moment, Tanner thought about interrupting, then realized the only way he would ever know just how bad it was between his dad and his brother was to eavesdrop, so he stopped just outside the doorway and listened. He could hear movement, then the clink of ice cubes in a glass. He frowned. It was damn early to be hitting the bottle. His father finally spoke, his voice raspy like it was whenever he drank whiskey.

"I'm not happy with Tanner. That fuckin' boy is too soft on those faggots. I'd think he was one of them if I didn't know he was raised better. He flat out isn't trying hard enough to disrupt things." There was another long pause. Tanner held his breath while he waited for Tim to reveal his suspicions, but his brother remained quiet.

"The general is scouting out an alternative site in Montana if we can't take care of this problem. Cartwright has to go. If we can't burn him out, then use whatever...or whoever you need to make sure he gets the message that his kind has no place around here. No safe place at all."

"Don't worry, Dad, if Tanner can't get the job done—I will."

"Good. Make like you're working with him for now, but I want your report in private. I won't tolerate cowardice or disloyalty."

Tanner took a few silent steps backward before once again approaching the study, making enough noise they would hear him coming. No one said a word. After retrieving his phone, Tanner returned to his room, and let the knowledge wash over him. The Trip-T was truly lost.

Chapter Four

Chad shuffled across the hard packed dirt toward the main house, a little stiff, but not too bad considering how much pain he'd been in the previous night. He resisted the urge to look around for the big cowboy, and ignored anything that resembled disappointment that the couch was empty and Jesse gone this morning. After all, he hadn't wanted the man there. And he certainly hadn't wanted the kiss. There was definitely not a little squiggly thrill thing happening in his stomach when he'd seen Jesse's sleeping bag and duffle propped against the wall in his living room.

With one quick look at the nearly empty yard, Chad stepped inside the back door and kicked off his sneakers. One thing about showing up late for breakfast, at least there wasn't a crowd. Jesse must already be out working on the ranch with all the other men. Not that he was thinking about the cowboy, because he wasn't. In fact, he should probably mention to Cass that Jesse needed a place to stay. Resisting the urge to beat his head against the door, Chad tried to think of a reason he could give Cass that he couldn't share his two-bedroom casita with someone. A reason other than he didn't do cowboys—and Jesse was more cowboy than anyone he'd ever met. *And he kissed me.*

"Little late for breakfast, Chad. Everything okay?" Ty's grin was wide, as he stood behind the stainless counter, and worked on arranging thinly sliced ham onto a tray already heavy with roast beef and salami.

"Yeah, I slept in a little. I had a flare up of an old injury."

"An old injury. Uh huh. Is that what you call it?"

"Call what?" Chad knew what Ty thought, but he wasn't going to play.

Ty shook his head. "Sorry, I wasn't sure anyone would crack your shell. I'm glad if the new guy does it for you—although I don't think he's the sticking around kind. For that matter, I wasn't sure you were, either...but here you are." Ty's smile was no longer teasing, and he looked genuinely pleased. "You better grab your coffee and head back. Cass is antsy to start the planning for the Ranch Quest day."

"Thanks, Ty." Chad was halfway to the dining room when Ty called out.

"Oh, hey, Chad? You might as well know, the guys had a little fun at your expense at breakfast, but your guy didn't give anything away."

"My guy? You mean Jesse? Oh, hell no. He just happened to be there when I hurt my back, and helped me home. It earned him a spot on the couch. There wasn't anything else."

Ty pressed his lips together as if he was trying not to laugh and turned away. Chad barely resisted the urge to stomp down the hall. Life could quickly go to hell if the men thought he had something going on with Jesse. Between the mess in Flagstaff and his own personal policy against cowboys, Chad just wasn't interested in dating anyone on the ranch. That would need to be something he cleared up at dinner tonight.

Loud laughter burst from Cass's office, and Chad was smiling as he stepped into the room, expecting to find the ranch owner and Holden bent over their respective computers. The smile faded when instead of working with the former sheriff, Cass was bent over a table and a pile of chart papers, head to head with Jesse Duran. The very man his brain insisted he didn't want to see, while everything below his neckline screamed *yes*. He cleared his throat, and both heads popped up.

"Hey there, sunshine." Warm brown eyes seemed to twinkle at him. Or maybe it was the way his smile seemed amplified by the deep lines bracketing his wide mouth. What would it feel like— Chad scowled.

Cass smiled at him, apparently unsurprised by Jesse's totally inappropriate greeting. "Good morning, Chad. You're just in time. We were getting ready to go over the plans for the Ranch Quest. Give us just a second to finish this."

Nodding in order to keep from snapping out his first response, Chad joined them at the table and scanned the top sheet. It was a scale drawing of the entire ranch. A red X marked the eastern-most boundary of the WSR. Cass took a red pen and made another X just to the north of the first mark.

"To give you a little more feel of the layout, here's where we were working to repair the cut fence and round up the strays yesterday, Jesse. I've got two former law enforcement types living on the ranch, but neither man is much of a cowboy, yet. And Holden is strictly forbidden from horses or the OHVs for now. Besides, he left this morning to help out with a little security problem in Needles. We were holed up until the wee hours trying to come up with a plan. Setting guards seems to be the only way to deal with the vandalism, except the ranch has a lot of fence to cover. There's no way the men can ride the fence line all night and work their regular chores during the day. Chance is heading in to Kingman to see if we can pick up a few extra hands to help out for a while. With the big event only weeks away, we don't want to take any chances with security."

Cass straightened and took a sip of his coffee. Turning his focus on Chad, he included him in the conversation. "With the extra hands we need to hire, I want to thank you for letting Jesse bunk with you while he's here."

Chad blinked. This must be like falling off a cliff. A slow motion moment where you think you can still save yourself if only you flail your arms fast enough. Protesting would only draw attention to his discomfort, besides, just because the man would be sleeping a room away didn't mean anything would happen. He wanted to show all the ranch hands just how indifferent he could be. Knowing he was going down, Chad found himself nodding in agreement, because damn if Cass hadn't come through and taken him in at the lowest moment of his life. And he could probably ignore the triumphant grin of the irritating cowboy with broad shoulders, narrow hips, and gentle kiss—if he tried really, really hard.

"So catch us all up, Chad," Cass said, apparently satisfied with the agreement and the security plans.

"Sure. Let me re-cap for Jesse's benefit. We have a daylong festival called Ranch Quest sponsored by Build-a-Dream. Twenty children and teens in various stages of treatment for life-threatening or terminal illnesses. This is strictly a one-day event, but it's important to put on a good show with the set up and dorms, because there will be representatives here from some of the week-long camps we want to sponsor in the future."

"What type of activities do you have planned?" Jesse asked. His brows were drawn into a frown as he looked down at the large map.

Cass pulled a second large scale drawing from the stack and laid it over the first, giving them a close up map of the main compound. Chad took a pad of sticky notes and a pen from Holden's desk and started marking the spaces to show where each activity would be set up. "This is where the vans will park. Ty wants to set up a food tent right here." He pressed the sticky down in a spot close to the house. "We're going to keep all the activities confined to the area between the main barn, the housing, and this paddock. That should keep everyone safe and make it easy to manage. The dorm under construction will be rough finished so we can give tours, but it will be roped off to prevent casual visitors from wandering through. We have two inflatable bounce houses and slides ordered, plus several large canopies to provide shade throughout the yard."

"You have a large open spot right here." Jesse pointed to a spot between the paddock and the housing area. Chad got lost for a moment at the sight of the broad hand and thick, calloused fingers.

A sip of coffee seemed like a really good idea, if he could keep from choking on it. "That's for a small petting zoo Drew is setting up. Drew Van, he's the local veterinarian and partner of Holden. Baby goats, lambs, and a pig, I think he said."

"This looks really good, Chad. What do you need help with?" Cass straightened and smiled down at him, and Chad suddenly felt like he was one of the little kids with these two cowboys towering over him. This was the part he'd been dreading, but the kids deserved this if they were coming to a ranch for the day.

He cleared his throat. "What I need is someone to set up a horseback ride and maybe a hayride. We only need one horse—you know, like the kind of rides they set up at carnivals? I know we don't have any ponies or anything but maybe you have a really gentle horse and someone who could walk one kid at a time around in a circle? He wouldn't have to be responsible for the kids, because they all have caretakers with them—" He was babbling, but he couldn't seem to stop. Standing between these two giant cowboys talking about horses brought all the nightmares and memories right to the surface.

Jesse seemed to sense his anxiety, because he dropped one big hand on Chad's shoulder and looked to Cass. "I don't know if you want me here for another three weeks, but if I can help, just say the word. Of course I don't know anything about kids…"

Chad laughed and hoped he was the only one who noticed the little note of hysteria that crept in.

"That makes us even—I don't know much about horses."

Jesse looked down at him, one eye squinting, as if skeptical. "How long have you been here?"

"Four or five months, I suppose." Chad shrugged up at the big man, trying not to look as stupid as he felt.

"You live on a ranch and you don't ride?"

"Yeah, well, horses and I don't exactly get along, okay?"

Dark eyebrows pulled together, Jesse frowned, making Chad feel even more like a little kid who had disappointed the grown ups. "If you got a problem with horses, you need be up front about it. Because it sounds to me like you plan to be all over this event." Jesse pointed to the map, glanced at Cass, then shifted his gaze back to Chad. "Even the gentlest of horses is likely to respond differently to someone who's afraid—so it would be better for all involved if you could reduce some of that anxiety."

Cass shifted his feet and turned to face Jesse. "You volunteering for those lessons? Because you'd have to stick around for sure. He'd need to spend some evenings in the stables, working the stalls, helping with the grooming and feed, making friends. Probably some horseback riding lessons involved, too." The unmistakable smile in Cass's deep voice grated against Chad's last nerve.

Jesse's wide mouth split into a grin. "Yeah, no worries…boss. I got this."

Chad hated them both.

****

Park looked at the stubborn set of his boss's jaw and knew there was no getting out of the investigation. To be fair, Janet didn't have a choice. When a complaint came to the Flagstaff office of Child Protective Services, CPS was bound by law to investigate. Truthfully, they *should* be required to investigate—for the sake of abused children everywhere. Park just wished they could have some sort of discretion when they were being used. And there was no doubt in his mind they were being used this time.

"Just listen," he asked once more.

With a tired sigh, Janet dropped her pen, removed her cheaters from their perch on the end of her nose, and rubbed her eyes. "I'm sorry, Park. Of course I'll listen. This is about that young teacher, right? Chad Ollom?"

"Yes. I investigated the original rumor last year—it didn't even merit a complaint—just a nasty whisper campaign. He was twenty-four, finishing up his Masters in Elementary Ed at NAU. He was a popular substitute around Coconino County. He never had a bad report, until one of the mothers at his prospective school discovered he was gay."

Janet picked up her tea and grinned. "This should be good—he a friend of yours?"

Park tossed his long blond hair back over his shoulder and batted his eyes. He added a little swish and lisp for effect. "Don't bust my balls, hon. Chad didn't know how to swang it, if you know what I mean."

Janet laughed, as he'd meant her to. She wasn't just his supervisor, they'd become friends, and she knew he'd have told her if there was a conflict of interest. They both relaxed into their seats, and Park took up the story again.

"Seriously, Janet—the boy was just about as straight as a queer kid can be. Not in the closet, he was in the Gay Alliance on campus, but he didn't go to meetings and never went out of his way to advertise it in any way that I could see—and it would have been inadmissible anyway. His orientation wasn't relevant to the complaint. Even so, it was during the period we were undergoing the court oversight, and Judge Turner ordered me to check. There was absolutely nothing obvious to offend the little one's mommies and daddies and no evidence whatsoever that he behaved inappropriately."

"Okay, I get it. Some conservative mom was offended by his sexuality and went overboard. That was almost a year ago. So why is this back— because we both know you're going to have to investigate—are you telling me there's been an official complaint? When was the last time Mr. Ollom was in a classroom in this county?"

"Exactly. He left the county to work on a private ranch in Mohave five months ago. But today, the father of a first grade boy stutters his way into my office with"—he used finger quotes—"*evidence* that his son was abused last year, when Ollom was a substitute."

Janet sat up straighter and put her glasses back on, suddenly all business. "A year ago? What's the evidence?"

Park looked down at the two Polaroid photographs, then handed them over. Janet looked at each photo, front and back, then pulled out a magnifying glass. Park knew Janet understood the situation immediately.

"He says these photos are from a spanking of a five-year-old boy? Administered by a teacher?" Her lips pressed together in a straight line.

Park nodded once.

"My left tit they are. Obviously, it's hard to prove from just these photos, but I just don't believe this bottom belongs to a kid, let alone a five-year-old. Does the father realize we are now obligated to investigate?"

"He does now, but Janet—" Park wanted to cry. "This is so unfair. Because now we have a barely six-year-old boy who's going to have to visit a doctor to show his bum, just so we can prove his daddy's a liar. Unless you can think of a better way to prove that's not this child's rear end."

Lowering her glasses once more, Janet nailed him with a look. "Why did he do this? What's going on that a father would put his son at risk to make this type of accusation? Is it possible Ollom really did do this and the father falsified evidence because he thought it was the only way to report the incident?"

"I asked him why he waited so long to report, because at first I wondered the same thing. He said unless he spoke up, Ollom was going to get away with *it*, and he didn't want *it* to happen to anyone else... He never once met my eyes. The bastard's lying—I don't know why. Who would put their own kid through something like this?"

Janet picked her pencil up and tapped it on the stack of file folders on her desk, her lips pursed into a little frown. Park winced, knowing he'd just added to her already overwhelming job. Guilt washed through him as he looked at the slump of her shoulders, her tired eyes, the prematurely silvered streaks that twisted through her dark hair. All the reasons why he had to leave. This job could kill a person.

Finally Janet blew out a breath and looked up at him. "Our hands are tied. Contact Mr. Ollom and request he come to our office within the next seventy-two hours. Contact Judge Turner and request a physical examination of the child—I want this one court ordered. Schedule the parents for an in-office interview. Unfortunately, until we have the results of the official exam, I can't authorize a home visit. Move quickly, Park, and document every single step along the way—I have a bad feeling about this one."

****

Chad ignored the chatter of the other two men and tried to avoid pouting, but dammit, Cass and Jesse didn't have to talk about him like he was a recalcitrant child. Who the hell did Jesse Duran think he was, anyway?

As if the man read his mind, Jesse's voice penetrated Chad's fog... "I'm an old rodeo cowboy who's been riding the circuit since I was fifteen as an amateur and seventeen as a pro. If you want me to put on a show for these kids, it wouldn't be too hard. Do you have access to rough stock?" Jesse grinned. "Make that a saddle bronc please...I don't want to find out you brought in a bull. I'm way too old for that shit."

Eight seconds, Chad. Just like a cowboy. That's not too much. You're eight years old, now, it's time to quit acting like a baby.

Chad closed his eyes and tried not to hear his father's voice. When the phone on his hip rang, Chad jumped and snatched it quickly from the leather holster.

"Ollom." He listened in stunned silence and waited for the earth beneath him to open up and swallow him whole. "I'll be there. Yes. I understand."

After ending the call, Chad gradually became aware of the silence in the room and looked up to find both men had stopped talking and were watching him.

"Chad? Is everything all right?" Cass moved close enough to put out his big hand and grip his shoulder. "Is your family okay?"

Blinking rapidly, trying to keep his vision clear, Chad had to swallow twice before he could speak. "That was CPS in Flagstaff. I have to report to their office day after tomorrow to make a formal statement and answer questions."

Cass squeezed his arm. "What the fuck? I thought that was all cleared up. They proved it was all just rumor. Shit. It's been half a year—why now?"

"There's been a new complaint...they say they have photos."

Jesse shuffled his feet, and Chad met his gaze, unable to think of a damned thing to say to convince this complete stranger that he hadn't hurt a child...that he would never—

"Stop, Chad. I'll have my attorney meet you there. I'll send Holden, too. He did a thorough background check. He wouldn't leave his son with you if there was even a hint you did this. It was some homophobe the last time, and it must still be related to that somehow. We *know* you didn't do this." Cass pulled him into a big bear hug. "You're part of our family now, Chad. We'll take care of this together."

Chapter Five

Dismounting quickly, Jesse kept Dabney's reins in one hand as he crossed the yard from the stables to the construction site. Chad was once again the only worker left in the yard, moving over the roof, testing boards, occasionally wielding his hammer, and focused only on what was in front of him. That was good. Jesse didn't want Chad to have much time to worry about what was coming next… Or from worrying about what Jesse had planned for later, either.

Jesse was no fool. He hadn't missed the shock when Cass announced the two of them would be roommates. Nor had he missed the slight slump of shoulders that telegraphed Chad's resignation. The younger man would try to make the best of what he undoubtedly considered an awkward situation. So be it. Jesse had made his own sacrifice last night when he'd put the other man to bed with just a kiss. Resisting the urge to rub his lips at the remembered sweetness of the moment, he decided not to think too hard about what that meant.

"Come on down, sunshine. You're finished with the construction for today, we've got more work to do tonight." Jesse kept his tone low, to keep from startling either the horse or Chad.

Chad's sigh carried clearly in the quiet yard, and Jesse bit back a smile. But apparently he'd given him a good enough sense of his stubborn streak the previous evening, because Chad started to gather his tools, then backed his way down the ladder. Jesse reached up and took the tool bucket as soon as Chad was close enough. The blond stopped two rungs from the bottom, leaving them nearly eye-to-eye.

"Look, I don't need you—"

Jesse spoke quietly over top of Chad's obvious aggravation. "Easy now. Got a friend of mine here I'd like you to meet."

Chad's mouth closed on a snap, and he leaned slightly to look around Jesse—although if he'd been focused on anything other than his anger, the fifteen-hand gelding would have been plenty visible. The man's golden tan faded into a pasty gray, and a light sheen of sweat appeared on his upper lip. "What are you doing?"

"I told you. Brought a friend. Come on down, and I'll help you clean up the construction site, then you can help me with Dabney, here."

Chad's knuckles whitened and his lips pressed into a tight line. "I've got a lot on my mind right now, Duran. I don't need any more stress."

"Exactly." Jesse turned away, keeping the reins in one hand and the bucket in the other. "Come on, Dabney needs to cool off, so we can walk the bucket over to our porch, then we'll take him back to his stall. Nice and easy. Just like walking a dog."

"Pretty big fucking dog." Chad mumbled the words, but Jesse thought there might have been a hint of a smile. He didn't give him any more time to think, just started walking with his tool bucket, maintaining a steady stream of casual conversation.

Setting the bucket on the edge of the porch, Jesse gave a look at Chad's tool belt. "Come on, drop your load and let's get this boy home." He patted the golden neck and received a soft, warm snort in return.

Looking into big brown eyes, Jesse stroked his hand over the white star on the horse's nose. "What's that, Dabs? No, I don't think it's personal. I'm sure he'll like you once he gets to know you." He bent his head closer and Dabney lipped the brim of his hat, then snorted and nodded his head.

Jesse laughed. "Come on, Chad. How can you say no to that?" Turning toward the barn, he was pleased to notice Chad fell into step beside him.

"I don't want to ride, Jesse."

"Do I look stupid? Wait—don't answer that. All I plan to do today is take Dabs back to his stall.

You can watch while I groom him. We'll fill his feed and be done. Okay?"

They spent a companionable few minutes moving through the barn, and Jesse noticed Chad had visibly relaxed once he'd realized there wouldn't be any pressure to ride. Someone had probably pushed him too hard and fast. Like those parents that threw their kid into the pool as a way to "teach" them to swim. It wasn't strictly necessary that Chad learn to ride for the Ranch Quest kids. After all, only those who were physically able would get on Dabney and be led once or twice around the paddock. But Jesse knew a thing or two about fear—and hell—even if he was going to take off in a few weeks, he couldn't stand to see something like that fester.

Jesse removed Dabney's bridle and bit, leaving only the head harness in place. "After our talk this morning, I asked around, then checked out the horses. Dabney here is perfect for what you need. He's got a steady, even gait that won't jar anyone unnecessarily. Easy on a lead, and I'm not sure anyone's ever told him he's a horse. Acts like a damn dog." He worked a few more minutes, feeling the weight of Chad's gaze on his back.

When he was finished, Jesse moved toward the stall door and Chad started back away. "Come'ere."

"No. Told you, I don't do horses." The blue eyes widened and he shook his shaggy blond head from side to side.

59

"Thank God for small favors. My dick's big, but it ain't that big. I'm afraid I'd shrivel if you got to comparing."

Chad blinked.

"It was a joke, Chad. Come on inside for just a second. You don't have to get on him." He held out his hand and waited, willing Chad to step forward, to beat back some of his crippling fear.

****

Chad stared at the outstretched hand. Tanned and broad across the knuckles, cracked, calloused — and open. Reaching out to bring Chad back from something that he'd allowed to rule his life for far too long. Not that fear of riding ruined his life — after the farm had been sold, there wasn't any real reason for him to be around horses. He'd certainly never planned to live on a ranch full of cowboys. But he couldn't deny the memories of his father or the nightmares that haunted his sleep. His hand seemed to make the decision independent of his brain, because he didn't remember reaching out, and yet, there was no refusing the rough comfort as the big man closed his fingers around Chad's and encouraged him to step into the stall.

Then his feet moved, too, and as if from a great distance, Chad watched as Jesse led him just inside the straw-covered stall until they stood next to the horse's front quarter. Dabney turned his head, his nostrils flaring, and he huffed out a soft breath.

Fear threatened to crawl up Chad's throat, making it hard to breathe. He might have tried to bolt if not for the big cowboy between him and the stall door. Jesse wrapped his arms around Chad's waist, his chest a light pressure against Chad's back.

"Hey, Dab's" Jesse's voice was whisper soft, and Chad had the strangest impression that was for his benefit, not the horse's. "This is my friend Chad." Jesse ran his hand up Chad's bicep then reached to stroke the sorrel neck. Again, the movement served to soothe both of them.

Without thinking first, Chad reached with trembling fingers to follow the path of Jesse's hand, the hot bristle under his fingertips, an unexpected sensory memory of happy times. "I used to like looking at the horses…"

"Yeah? Did you grow up around horses?" Jesse's voice was almost hypnotic, coaxing long-buried remembrances of lazy summer days, the smell of horseflesh and leather, of men and sweat, of hay and dust. And the memories of a little boy whose inner fears warred with his need to make his daddy proud.

Standing this close to the big animal made his throat tighten, but having Jesse pressed lightly against his back made it bearable. Maybe he could…explain. At least a little. "Yes. A small Quarter Horse farm in northern New Mexico."

Unsure he wanted to share more than that, Chad pulled his hand back and hugged himself. The cowboy followed his movement and placed his big hand over Chad's, so that they wrapped together around his waist. An awkward comfort. Realizing that Jesse was going to let him tell it at his pace, Chad took a deep breath, nodded, and decided to continue his story.

"My dad was a big man, tried rodeo for a bit, but always said he was too tall to ride bulls, and money wasn't good enough to ride anything else. Honestly, he probably wasn't good enough, but it was years before I was born. He and my mom got married when she got pregnant with me, and they bought a little place outside Tucumcari."

Apparently growing bored with either the story or the lack of attention, Dabs, snorted, then bent his head and began to eat. In the confined space, Chad had an up close and personal look at big teeth grinding down, and it wasn't hard to imagine a crushing bite to his hand if he got too close. Jesse tightened his arms, holding Chad steady when he would have stepped back.

Warm breath ruffled his hair and tickled his ear. "It's okay. Dabs won't mind if we hang out with him a little longer."

"Yeah. Okay. Uhm... We weren't a big operation, but then my dad had a horse—Rajun'—who became a bit of a local legend and his stud fees carried the farm. The horse scared me—all of them did, really. Obviously, I'm not a big man, and as a kid I was always the smallest in my class, for my age group. Mom said it was okay—I'd grow. I take after her family.

"Dad could see I was scared and he hated it— was always bringing me along to watch the cowboys. Rodeos, training sessions on the farm, other ranches—no matter where we went, he made it a point to put me right in the middle of the livestock with him. The horses always seemed huge..."

"Did he make you ride?"

"Not much, because Mom wouldn't let him at home. But whenever she wasn't around, he'd make me get up on the other cowboys' horses. On my eighth birthday, he decided that was enough. He put me on Rajun' and slapped his haunch."

"Aww, shit. What happened?"

Chad shrugged. "About what you expect. Rajun' took off—I screamed—Rajun' went faster." He paused, gathering his thoughts. He swallowed around an unexpected lump in his throat, the sting in his eyes surprising.

"We went about a quarter mile, heading straight toward a storm. I...uh...I don't remember much. Lightning struck right close, and Rajun' reared up. I landed in some two-strand. Took three surgeries and a full year to teach me to walk again."

Jesse pulled him into a tighter embrace, offering comfort for a remembered hurt. "I'm sorry that happened, Chad."

"I think that's the first time you've called me by my name." His smile hovered a minute, then he pressed forward. Maybe it would help to get it all out there. He sucked in a shuddering breath. "They had to put Rajun' down. Dad had borrowed against the next year's stud fees. Six months after the accident my dad killed himself and my mom sold the farm."

The weight of his confession left him breathless, shivering despite the heat of the late afternoon barn. Jesse turned him around and lifted his chin.

"Nothing, Chad. Look up at me. You have nothing to be ashamed of, nothing to feel bad about."

Chad nodded, but could only meet the dark eyes for a minute before he dropped his gaze. "Logically, I do know that. Seven and eight year old children aren't responsible for their parent's decisions. It's part of why I wanted to be a teacher." He sucked in another breath. "But I can't help but wonder what life would have been like if I had just gotten on the damned horses when he'd wanted me to, you know?"

Jesse cupped Chad's face in his big hands, and rubbed a thumb over his lower lip. The gesture was so…odd. Unexpected. For a moment, Chad thought he really might cry. He'd just revealed his most tightly guarded secret to this virtual stranger and found…comfort. Slowly he dragged his gaze upward, over the tight T-shirt, grimy from the day's work, along the curve of bicep, all sinew and strength. The same strong features he'd noticed earlier, now felt somehow different. The strong jaw, dark with a two-day stubble, wide mouth underneath a decidedly crooked nose—as if it had been broken more than once—dark brown eyes under ridiculously heavy lashes.

With his face still cradled by the other man, Chad put one hand on Jesse's forearm, holding him in place while he reached with the other to trace along the line that bracketed Jesse's mouth. The cowboy's face was so serious that the normal crinkles around his eyes relaxed, revealing a fan of white lines. What would he look like completely relaxed? Sleeping? Chad blinked at the idea of waking up next to the bigger man. His dick filled at the thought.

Needing a taste, Chad parted his lips and licked Jesse's thumb. The salt and grime from the day exploded across his taste buds, a tantalizing appetizer from a forbidden fruit. Jesse moaned softly and pressed his cheek into Chad's hand. The moment stretched out, then Jesse's voice rasped out.

"Damn." Lowering his head, Jesse waited until their lips were scant inches apart before he pulled his thumb from Chad's mouth with a pop and replaced it with his lips. The kiss was electric. A sudden squall, turning their peaceful moment into a tempest of need that had both men groaning. Their teeth bumped as they moved their mouths, seeking that perfect angle to deepen the kiss despite the difference in their heights. Jesse pulled back long enough to curse again. "Damn. Closer."

Claiming his mouth once more, Jesse dropped his hands to Chad's waist and lifted, and Chad wrapped his legs around the taller man's waist. The new position was hot, leaving Chad's erection pressed hard enough against the zipper to leave marks. Jesse turned and moved them both backward until Chad's back pressed against the stall. *Jesus, that no cowboys, no horses resolution sure left in a hurry.*

He realized it was the first time someone had manhandled him without making him feel less than a man. He knew his small stature and young features were a turn on for some guys. It had always made him feel squicky—as if he was feeding into some pedophile fantasy. It had kept him safely out of stranger sex and more into the buddy fuck range. There was nothing about Jesse's touch that left him feeling uncomfortable—this man was willing to move him any way he needed to in order to get at what he wanted. And what he wanted right now was apparently Chad's dick.

Chad leaned his hips back slightly to provide better access. He held his breath as the big man worked at his zipper, but Jesse was careful to avoid catching anything important in the steel teeth. Jesse's teeth were another matter, because even as his hands were busy at Chad's crotch, his mouth moved from their kiss to trail small nips and bites along Chad's neck. All he could do was arch into the dual sensations and moan his desire.

Jesse stretched the elastic waistband of Chad's underwear and eased his cock out, then circled his hand around Chad's length. "Nice," he murmured against Chad's collarbone. He stroked him a few times before swirling his thumb into the bead of pre-cum and spreading it over the tip.

"Shit, my hands are rough." While his tongue and teeth continued to work at Chad's neck, Jesse put his palm in front of Chad's mouth, and—oh fuck that was hot—Chad slicked the big hand with his own spit. Jesse gripped him, nice and firm, just as he liked it—no limp hand action for him—and began to stroke, fast, with an edge of desperate. Chad rocked into the motion, each movement dragging a puff of breath from his lungs, like a locomotive blowing off steam.

"Come for me now, and we'll take this back to our place and do it right."

It was as if Jesse had flipped a switched with the words *our place*. In this position with all his clothes scrunched around the important parts, Chad cried out and thought he would orgasm without coming—then his ass muscles clenched hard, his balls drew up tight, and cum pumped, spilling over Jesse's hand and soaking the front of their clothes.

"Damn…" Jesse breathed out, then pressed their foreheads together. "That was beautiful."

"Let me make sure my legs still work and I'll—"

"Jesse? You in here?" Whit's voice was like an alarm calling from the front of the barn.

Jesse placed a finger over Chad's mouth, before he answered. "Just finishing up, be right there. What's up?" Jesse quietly lowered Chad to the floor, holding on to his shoulders, checking to make sure he really could stand.

"Cass needs to see all the hands in the office. He sent me to ask if you could come, too."

Keeping steady eye contact, Jesse waggled his brows at Chad, nearly surprising a laugh out of him. "Yeah, I'd like to come, too."

"Later," he whispered. He kissed the top of Chad's head, then with a rueful grin, wiped his hand on the bandana he pulled from his back pocket, and headed back out into the barn.

It wasn't until many minutes passed before Chad realized he was alone with Dabney. Still smiling, he chanced a pat on the horse's rump, then adjusted his pants and left for home.

Chapter Six

Jesse held the reins loosely as he scanned the moonlit horizon for anything out of place. Pinion and juniper scented the air, and with no moon, the sky wore the Milky Way like a sash. They'd been riding for close to four hours and Angel still moved easily under the saddle. Apparently the ornery horse favored late night rides on the open range.

He patted the big black neck, feeling the faint hint of sweat. "Last of our assigned check points, big fella. Don't worry, I won't tell anyone how well you behaved."

Shifting uncomfortably, Jesse opened his fly and adjusted himself. Again. "Same to you, big guy." Laughing, he looked around at the empty landscape. "Great. Now I'm talking to my dick." He couldn't decide whether he was more amused because he was talking out loud in the middle of the night with no one but his horse to hear...or because he'd called his own dick *big guy*.

With a final look over his shoulder at the empty landscape, Jesse was struck by just how futile his assignment really was. The ranch itself was ten thousand acres of empty land, with an additional fifteen thousand leased from the federal and state governments. He wasn't exactly sure how many linear miles they were talking about, but even split up across the property, with only six men available on a shift, trying to claim they were any type of a deterrent was just foolish.

As soon as they turned south, Angel's ears pricked up and his gait seemed to have a little extra bounce.

"Yep, I'm ready to be home too, Angel. It's been a hell of a long night. Soon as we get there you can have a nice cool drink and we'll both grab some shut eye."

Over the course of the evening and into the night, Jesse had maintained a constant scan of the surroundings, his focus trained primarily at the dark shapes of the trees and occasional glimpses of fence lines that made up the border of the WSR property boundaries. Now, he thought he could relax a little as they headed toward the interior of the ranch. Another hour—maybe less—and they'd be home. He shifted once again and scanned the horizon, wondering how long before he caught a glimpse of the lights from the houses and barn.

As he stared a little unfocused and a whole lot tired, there was a sudden flare, a distant flash of yellow-orange exploded on the horizon. *Fuck.* He squeezed Angel's sides, urging his mount to pick up the pace. Something very big in the direction of the compound was burning and not one single happy explanation came to mind.

****

By the time Chad dressed and ran out the door, he knew any hope of saving the new dorm was lost. The roof and frame were fully engulfed, spitting sparks twenty feet high, as the hungry flame looked for its next victim. Fire was every rancher's nightmare out here in the Arizona desert. Outside the immediate vicinity of the living quarters, fire suppression was handled on a case-by-case basis, each wildland fire evaluated for cause and conditions. In the old days, every fire was put out as soon as possible, before it ate away too many acres of forested land. Now, fires were often left to burn, if the cause was natural and there was no immediate danger to life or property. Lightning was just another tool in maintaining nature's balance.

The roar from the fire was in discordant harmony with the rushing sound in his own head as Chad raced across the yard toward the barn, and the sickening sound of a horse's scream. He saw Juan and Kerry already firing up the water truck, and knew the two of them would be working the pump, emptying the holding tank before switching to well water to spray on the flames. Although the barn was a good distance from the destroyed dorm, the breeze carried burning ash and smoke, creating a sense of urgency among man and horse. There wasn't any place to put a personal thought for safety, no room for fear—just time for action.

Inside the barn, horses snorted and stomped, some moving restlessly, others close to panic. Chad looked around, trying to figure out how he could be the most help. Behind him the heavy main doors swung closed with a loud bang, muting some of the outside noise, and shielding the horses from the sight of the flames.

"Open the stall doors, we're steering them toward the paddock, they'll be fine there," Whit shouted. He fitted word to action and began to work the left side of the barn, trusting Chad to do likewise. He wasted no time, just went to the first stall, released the latch, then stood back as a golden horse with a white ass raced from the stall, heading straight for the opposite end of the barn, and the cool night air.

Working quickly, Chad went to the next stall, and then the next. He was grateful he didn't have to let Angel out of his stall, since he and several other horses were out with the men working tonight. *Oh, hell.*

"Whit? Has anyone radioed Jesse and the others? Have we heard from them?"

Whit's face was grim and he moved to the last stall on his side. "Don't know. You got the last two stalls over there? I'm going to head to the paddock, see if I can't calm these boys and girls down. Go find Cass—see if everyone's okay."

Whit went through the open door as Chad released the last two latches. Dabney stood and looked at him for a long moment, as if he was uncertain he should leave Chad alone. "It's okay, boy—you head on out. Everything's going to be all right." As if the damn horse understood every word he said, Dabs nodded his head then left the barn on a trot.

Chad believed what he'd told the horse, as if that made a difference. Unless there was a huge shift in the wind, it was unlikely the falling ash could ignite the barn. Cass practiced smart fire prevention, no dried brush anywhere near the buildings, all buildings far enough apart to reduce the risk of a fire jumping structures, and he had a water tanker in the main compound, and the men kept it topped off with a fanatical fervor.

Chad followed Whit and the horses out the paddock side door, then climbed over the fence to head back to the fire fighting. From the looks of things, the fire was contained, if not yet out. The men had two hoses trained on the blaze, at both the front and the back of the dorm. Because the interior had yet to be finished, the bitch fire had fed from the outside walls, causing the entire building to collapse in on itself. Acrid smoke hung heavy in the air, burning his nostrils, and clogging his throat. He blinked rapidly against the sting and tried to blame it all on the smoke. They would have to start the dorm over, but at least the horses were safe. He hoped to God the men standing watch tonight fared as well. Chad wiped the sweat from his face and turned toward the two men standing near the rear of the tanker. Ty and Cass.

Voices carried as he moved closer.

"There is no sense in calling anyone out tonight," Cass said.

There was a long pause, and Chad realized Cass must be talking on the phone. He hesitated, not wanting to intrude, but Cass waved him over with his free hand.

"No. I got that. Yeah, I'll call in the morning." Another pause. "I promise. Okay see you in the morning." Cass disconnected and slipped the phone into the pocket of his jeans.

"What did Holden say?" Ty asked.

Although not quite as tall as Cass, Ty always seemed bigger to Chad, probably because he was built like an inverted triangle stuck on top of two tree trunks. When he was standing in his kitchen wearing a white chef's apron—the dark hair, blue eyes—Ty was like a walking wet dream. If you went for the silent-but-deadly type. Not that Chad did, but he didn't mind looking. Most of his dates had been with the geeky academics that seemed to populate the Education Department at NAU. Of course, he didn't go for the cowboy types either, he reminded himself. Which brought him right around to the reason he'd raced over here.

"He agrees in principle nothing is to be gained bringing anyone out tonight, but we still have to call it in so they can investigate and file the report. This is going to bring out the insurance investigator, too. That's who I have to call in the morning."

"Have you heard from Jesse?" Chad interrupted. "I mean from any of the guys out there? Are they okay?" He gestured vaguely, while he searched Cass's face for clues.

"Hey, I'm okay," the already all-too-familiar voice said from behind him. Chad spun around and found himself face-to-chest with Jesse. Big arms reached around him and they hugged tightly for a moment. Chad melted into the embrace, closing his eyes and resting his head against Jesse's broad chest. His own pulse rose to meet the rapid beat of Jesse's heart rate, and then he was drowning in sensation. Right at that moment, everything between them seemed to fit.

Stunned by his body's apparent recognition of a mate, Chad stepped back, distancing himself from the cowboy, more disturbed than he could say by the overwhelming relief that flooded through him at the knowledge Jesse was safe.

Chad turned back to face Cass, trying to slow whatever false signals his body was trying to send. "What about the others? Is everyone okay?"

Jesse stepped up behind him and draped his arms around Chad's shoulder.

Cass looked toward the dorm, his eyes narrowed, mouth a grim line. "Everyone has returned. Jesse was the last—they're all safe." He nailed Jesse with a look. "You didn't see anything out there?"

"Not a goddamn thing. Except this." Jesse jerked his head toward fire. "I can give you the exact time it went up, but that's about it. There was no sign of any one in my direction."

"Yeah same story from everyone. Okay…" Cass stared over at the fire for a minute. "Ty baby, these guys are gonna be at this several more hours yet. How about you get us a pot of coffee and some sandwiches? Do you mind?"

Ty narrowed his gaze and leveled a look at his lover. "That depends. You aren't thinking about doing something stupid like mounting a search party as soon as I step away, are you? Because that would piss me off…"

Cass laughed softly. "Easy, lover. Everyone stays in the compound until the sheriff gives us the all clear in the morning. I assume he'll want to talk with the men who rode patrol. Chad, you're staying in Flag tomorrow night, right? What time are you heading out—in case there are questions about the construction."

"Oh…uh…" Fuck. He'd forgotten all about the interview with CPS. With little sidesteps, he moved away from Jesse once again, already turning toward his casita. "I should leave by noon, I suppose. My appointment is first thing Thursday morning. "

"All right. My attorney will meet you there. I'll try to make sure Holden is freed up and available to leave with you—otherwise he'll have to travel later.

"No, don't do that," Chad said.

Cass's gaze strayed to Jesse, then back to Chad.

"No. Cass—just stop. You and Ty can stop babying me, okay? I appreciate the lawyer, but Holden is going to be plenty busy and...uhm, I don't need anything. Really. At least not until I know what they're accusing me of. I'm going to get my work boots and go help with the fire. See you all later." Chad walked the short distance to his casita, feeling their heavy stares like a weight on his back.

****

Tanner pulled to a stop in front of the house, put the truck in park, then folded his arms over the steering wheel and rested his head. The lights in his father's den meant he was out of time but he wanted just a few minutes to compose his thoughts before reporting his success.

The fire hadn't been hard to set. Every ranch had the perfect ingredients stored in a hundred different places. It was just a matter of finding what he wanted and arranging it to look like as much like an accident as possible. Everything he'd used had been small quantities, and, with the exception of a variety of cigarette butts he'd picked up at the I-40 rest area, everything had belonged to the WSR.

The fire had started slowly, and by the time the slow drizzle of fuel found the small open flame generated by the bale of hay and the cigarettes...well, Tanner had been well away from the ranch. The fire investigator would be hard-pressed to find any hard evidence of arson. One thing he could say about working with the general and the rest of his paranoid nutjobs...they sure had domestic terrorism down to a science.

Tanner swallowed around the sudden wash of bile that threatened. Tonight had been a major test...in more ways than one.

Now it was time to go inside and what he wanted more than anything was to tell his dad to count him out. Climbing from the cab of the truck, Tanner closed the door and leaned against the warm metal, looking up. Billions of stars millions of miles away cut a wide swath through the dark sky, making him feel small, insignificant, and very much alone. With a heavy sigh, Tanner straightened and, with feet made of lead, moved slowly toward the door. He took one long look over his shoulder and wondered if this would be the last night he'd ever see. All he wanted was out...

"About damn time you made it home. What the hell happened out there? You didn't think you should call and check in?"

Tanner walked to the sideboard and poured himself two fingers of scotch. "Don't you read your own manuals, Dad?" He took a sip and let the amber fluid burn its way down his throat and land in his stomach with all the subtlety of a dropped anchor. "The key to covert operations is to make everything appear as normal as possible—remember that part? I don't normally make calls after ten at night—I sure as hell don't want there to be any activity on my phone records that could be added to a pile of circumstantial evidence."

Trip snorted. "Don't smart ass me, boy. What the hell happened?"

Tanner moved to the doorway. "You might as well come in and make yourself comfortable, Tim." He'd seen T-bone through the window with his dad when he'd pulled into the drive and knew there was no way his younger brother wouldn't be listening.

With his lip curled in his permanent snarl, T-bone sauntered across the room and joined their father on the couch. "Okay, big brother, impress me. Tell me how you did without me along to take care of your mess. What did you do, cut another fence?"

Tanner knew better than to take the bait. No way would he admit to anything directly in front of either of them. He no longer accepted the idea that family came first. Not with them—they had an agenda that he just wasn't a part of.

"There was a fire at the WSR tonight. Rumor has it…the big new bunkhouse they were building mighta burned to the ground in some sort of accident."

"Huh. You did that? And you think burning down an unoccupied half-built building is going to convince Cartwright to sell the WSR?"

Leveling a look at his brother, Tanner gave him the truth. "No, I don't think anything is going to convince Cass to sell. Everything about your plan is a bad idea. He's got a couple of former cops living onsite. We already know they're willing to overlook rules to protect their own. He has a good place, he's doing what he wants, he's going to fight to keep it."

"They are an abomination! Queers and child molesters. A threat to God-fearing men and women."

"I don't know, Daddy. I think Tanner doesn't mind what they're doing out there. Maybe he's one of them?"

"That's enough, Timothy. If I thought one of my own children was a queer, I'd kill him myself." His father turned back to face him, and Tanner kept the mask in place. "Now, you listen here, Tanner. If you're right and we haven't found the right motivation, then we need to work harder. Things are in place and I believe the pedophile will be gone by Thursday. You tell me Cartwright's people are what's most important to him, then you start taking them away. One-by-one. And Tanner, if you won't do it, Timothy will."

Chapter Seven

Streaks of peach and pink streaked the sky by the time Chad was relieved from his duty with the hose and shovel. The fire was down to burning embers and lazy drifts of smoke when Whit and Juan ordered everyone to take a break. Showers, breakfast, and then the chores. There were horses to tend to, animals to feed, fencelines to inspect. Everyone had something to do. Everyone except Chad.

There were only two main jobs he had on the ranch. They kept him busy from sunrise to sunset, and left him feeling both accomplished and tired enough to sleep at the end of every day. Monday through Thursday, the mornings were set aside for teaching first grade to Holden and Drew's son, Alex. In the afternoons and on weekends he worked his ass off overseeing the new construction projects. The dorm had been the latest and most ambitious of the new buildings. And now it was nothing but a pile of smoldering rubble. With this week serving as their spring break, Alex had been riding along with his dads, so Chad didn't even have the morning in the classroom to distract him.

Chad glanced over toward his house and saw no sign of life—no lights, no movement behind the windows. Since Cass declared a mandatory rest for all the men who'd been riding patrol before the fire, Chad had been spared facing Jesse for the last three hours. Now, the cowboy's presence loomed large.

Gawd...had he really climbed up on the man like a spider monkey for a hand job? In a horse stall, no less... He shook his head and dragged his feet through the ash and dust, crossing the yard as slowly as possible, while crossing his fingers the man was gone. Or unconscious. Because sure as shit, Chad knew if they hadn't been interrupted, he'd have been on his knees with his mouth wide open—or even worse—he'd have been begging that cowboy to take him for a ride.

That was the last thing he needed to complicate his life. All this shit hanging over him in Flagstaff was bad enough, but Chad wasn't stupid. There would definitely be an insurance investigation because of the fire—and he'd been the one in charge of construction. He'd already lost one career because of circumstances beyond his control, now the fall back job could be in trouble, too.

Maybe Jesse would be gone from their casita. Or perhaps Chad could sneak in, grab a quick shower and a nap before his drive to Flagstaff. Whatever—he just knew he wasn't ready to face the cowboy. Not today.

Chad opened the door and stepped inside. He blinked rapidly, allowing his eyes to adjust to the dim light before heading toward his room. He took two steps when a sound behind him made him stop.

"Hey." The voice was rough, sleepy. Sexy. "Everything okay over there?"

"Yeah. It's just about done—a couple of guys still hanging around but they sent me home. Everyone else seems to have their own chores to do." Hell. He hadn't intended to share his inner musings.

Jesse sat up, his sleeping bag a rumpled heap on the couch. He raked his fingers through his hair, leaving it standing on end. In his wrinkled white T-shirt and sleepy eyes the cowboy looked like something out of a wet dream.

"Well I guess that just gives us time to do what I had in mind today," Jesse said.

The blood went straight to Chad's dick, and he barely resisted the urge to adjust himself. "Oh...uh... I thought I'd get a little sleep before I have to head out of town."

Jesse stood and stretched his arms high above his head. In the space between the hem of his shirt and the top of his boxers Chad caught a good look at the dark treasure trail leading below the waistband. His mouth went a little dry. Jesse dropped his hands to his waist and twisted his back from side to side, little cracks and creaks of joints punctuating the movement. "Naw, where's the fun in that? Grab yourself a quick shower and put on some jeans. We're going to take a horse ride. I got the picnic already packed." With that surprising news Jesse turned and sauntered toward the kitchen. "I'll start the coffee, you get that shower."

Unable to think of any thing else to do or say, Chad followed orders and headed to his room.

Thirty minutes later Chad felt the heat rise in his cheeks as Jesse gave him a foot up into the saddle. "Okay, tell me the truth here, Chad. Did you ever do any riding when you were little? I mean before…"

"Yeah. We had a pony that plodded around the paddocks. I used to ride him when I was five and six. It wasn't until I got a little older and my dad started talking about putting me on one of the big cutters that I freaked out."

"Good—it's just like riding a bicycle. You've probably got some muscle memory that you don't even know about. All we're going to do today is take a short ride out to a little spot I found, have a picnic, and head back. Nothing you need to worry about, because Dabs knows what he's doing. Jesse patted the beautiful chestnut colored neck and then handed Chad the reins. "Steer him like he's a car."

With those surprising and less than helpful directions, Jesse untied Angel, put his boot in the stirrup and swung the other leg over his horse's broad back.

For the first ten minutes Chad's stomach threatened to give up the coffee he'd sucked down before they'd left the house. He felt awkward, as his hips seemed to move in one direction while his shoulders wanted to go in the other. Twice his foot slipped from the stirrup and Chad grabbed the horn on the front of the saddle hanging on for dear life while he fished around with his foot until he found purchase. He knew Jesse was watching him but the big man never said a word and never laughed. Obviously, he had remarkable restraint when he wanted.

"Here we are. I'm going to tie Angel over there then come back and help you down." Jesse put action to word, and Chad admired the slim hips in the faded jeans as Jesse moved all loose limbed and comfortable in his skin. Then he frowned. He didn't want the man to treat him like some helpless kid.

The long ago memory served him well as he gripped the reins in one hand, shifted his hips, then put his weight on his left foot. Standing in the stirrup, he swung his other leg over Dabney's back and lowered himself to the ground. With a firm grip on the saddle, Chad tested gravity and was pleased to discover that despite the shakiness, his legs would in fact support his weight. For a moment he was prepared to gloat. Then Dabney snorted and it sounded too close to a laugh for comfort.

"Shut up, smart ass," he muttered under his breath. "We made it didn't we?" Actually, he was surprised to realize they'd been riding nearly a full hour. At some point, he'd stopped thinking about every step and the chance of falling and started to enjoy the leisurely pace through the surrounding rangeland. They'd come to a stop in a dip in the landscape too small to be called a valley—just a low spot between two small hills and surrounded by heavy old juniper trees with limbs that brushed the ground. The effect a natural shelter, a shield from prying eyes—not that there were any out here.

"Hey, great, you're down and moving. You tie Dabney over there, leave his reins nice and long, so he can eat, but not so long that he tangles himself up." Jesse lifted a small bundle from his saddlebag. "I'm gonna set this stuff out."

Chad did as instructed, pleased at the trust, then hung back watching as Jesse spread a blanket on the ground. Opening a thermos, Jesse poured a cup of coffee and took a small sip before resealing the top. Looking up, he met Chad's gaze.

"I won't say I don't bite, but come over here anyway." Jesse's smile was easy, relaxed, and when he took another sip of coffee, Chad wanted to share the taste straight from Jesse's lips.

Instead he pointedly looked from Dabney to Angel, then down at the blanket. "Why are you doing this?"

One eyebrow quirked up, and a wide grin split Jesse's face. "Maybe I have designs on that goddamn delicious-looking beautiful butt." He grabbed something from the blanket and threw it. Chad caught it right at his chest, looked down, and couldn't resist laughing.

"You have designs on my ass but you bring me Twinkies for breakfast? Seriously?"

"Hey, I never said I could cook. And it's the thought that counts. Come on, have a seat." Jesse added a spot on the blanket.

Taking a seat just a little out of range on the small blanket wasn't easy, but Chad wanted an answer to his question before anything happened between them. Making a show of opening the cellophane wrapper, he removed one of the sponge cakes. "Talk to me. You got me on a horse, something I never thought I'd do again. You brought me this gourmet breakfast. And if it wasn't for the fact you were hogging the coffee, I might actually think you cared. So tell me why."

Jesse's grin widened as he took another sip of coffee. He poured more into the cup and handed it to Chad. His gaze wandered over to Dabney as the silence stretched between them. When he finally answered, his voice was quiet in the stillness of the morning. "Fear is an ugly thing. It can eat away at you—just like any cancer. It seemed to me you'd lived with this long enough." He turned his head and met Chad's gaze. "Not the answer you were expecting, huh?"

"No, I can't say that it was. I sort of thought this was an elaborate scheme to take advantage of me."

Jesse threw his head back and laughed, the sound bouncing around their secluded site. When he finally stopped laughing, he wiped the tears from his eyes. "God. You are so fucking cute. In case you forgot, I had your dick in my hand. Nature being what it is, if we hadn't been interrupted, I'm pretty damn sure the next step would have been *my* dick in something of yours. I expect when you walked in the door this morning, all you could think about was bad shit—understandable—you've got a lot on your mind."

Chad realized he was nodding in agreement. His thoughts had been pretty bleak. He'd only wanted to be left alone so he could—what? Wallow in his own stink?

"See there? You just realized you hadn't thought about any of that stuff for the last hour. Sometimes you just have to get out of your own head. So you got out, overcame the one thing that had been holding you back since you were a kid. I know I don't have all the details about what's going on in Flagstaff, but you're going to overcome that situation too."

Chad nodded again, then cleared his throat. "Thanks." He shook his head. "Thanks," he said in a stronger voice. "You're right, this ride—getting on the horse—was something I never thought I'd do. This gave me a measure of control and was exactly what I needed this morning." He blew out a breath, then found a genuine smile for Jesse.

Returning the smile, Jesse nodded. "Now, I'm not bragging or anything, but I'm pretty damn confident that even with everything on your mind I could've found a distraction for you in your shower this morning. But this..." He gestured upward, and Chad followed the movement of his hand.

Looking up toward the cloudless blue sky, the varied greens of the pinions and junipers, Chad's breath hitched in his throat at the beauty of the morning. When had this rough landscape begun to feel like home?

Jesse shifted, rose up, coming closer. "Yeah...you get it. Now, about that other thing..." His grin was positively feral as he stalked on hands and knees.

Barely suppressing a laugh, Chad leaned forward, like he was going to meet Jesse for a kiss. His heart pounded wildly, and the muscles in his belly tightened before he gave in to the laughter and stuffed a Twinkie into Jesse's mouth.

With a grunt of surprise, Jesse captured his hands and rolled them both over, so that Chad was suddenly wearing the big cowboy. The moment stretched, as Jesse looked down at him, his dark eyes gleaming, then he lowered his mouth to

Chad's, the yellow cake hovering for a moment before Jesse mashed the two of them together in a messy mix of lips, tongue, cake, and cream filling.

Their kiss was long, and oh-so-sweet, as Jesse pinned Chad's head between his forearms, while he licked at the sweet mess. The kiss spun out, both of them making small, satisfied sounds, their hips beginning to rock together.

"Want you," Jesse murmured against his mouth.

All Chad could do was moan as Jesse's words went straight to his cock, jerking his hips upward in obvious approval.

Rising up on his knees, Jesse pulled off his shirt, then unbuckled his belt before opening the button fly. He hitched and pushed until the jeans came off, then he helped Chad do the same, until they were both naked. Chad explored with his eyes, taking in every detail.

Nothing in his past experience had prepared him for the potent sexuality of the man who even now towered over him. Everything about this moment felt raw, wild, made him hungry for something he hadn't realized he wanted. Sure he'd had lovers in the past. Men who were not exactly closeted so much as they were discreet. Friends from the education department, future or current teachers and administrators, who, like him, preferred to keep their personal and professional lives separate. Their liaisons had been carefully orchestrated, a movie or dinner out, followed by a return to one of their apartments. Safe. Private. Perfectly adequate. Nothing…no one to compare to this living-life-out-loud cowboy.

Faded bruises and a smattering of small scars covered Jesse's ribs and chest, and Chad vowed to explore each one—along with the furred chest, the flat, dark nipples, the hard, wiry muscles of his pecs and biceps. Later. Much later. Right now, the only thing he wanted was that beautiful cock inside him. Oh—

"Shit—Jesse—hang on. I can do without slick, but please tell me you have a condom in your bag of tricks?"

Jesse reached for his jeans, dug around in a pocket, then tossed a couple of packets of lube and condoms onto the blanket. "Wasn't a Boy Scout, but I'm always prepared."

"Big plans, too." Chad barely got the words out before Jesse captured his mouth in another mind-searing kiss. Jesse shifted them again, using his knee to encourage Chad to spread his thighs, while his hands were busy with the packets and rolling on a condom. As their tongues tasted and explored, Chad felt his ass cheeks spread apart and a lube-slick finger brush over his hole. Moaning with the heat of it, Chad opened his legs further and dropped his knees wide apart.

The finger tap-tapped at his entrance and a shiver coursed through him, rocking them both with the strength of his response to the light touch. Jesse laughed softly, then moved his mouth to scrape whiskers against Chad's neck before biting down hard.

"Oh fuck, yes." Chad arched and writhed, seeking more touch, more heat. The finger became more insistent, pressing, tapping, pushing against the tight muscle but never quit breeching his hole. Chad rocked his hips, trying to anticipate, but somehow the cowboy was always half a move ahead.

"Mmm…please…I need, Jesse. Don't tease…"

"Stay with me. My hands are rough, gonna go nice and slow. Don't worry, I got you."

Fingers traced along his crease, then moved softy around his pucker, almost-there presses that loosened the tight ring of muscles without opening him. Infuriating, maddening, teasing touches. Closing his eyes, Chad went with the sensations, gave up the illusion that he had any control over what Jesse was doing to him. As he surrendered conscious control, his body relaxed into the caress.

The muscles low in his belly felt it first—a slow, melting warmth that rippled, passing the message along to the muscles in his ass, down his thighs. Through it all, Jesse alternated bites, kisses, and licks, his attention evenly spread between Chad's mouth and his dick. An erotic overload of unexpected tenderness that was unraveling every bit of his protective web of self-preservation. The tiny part of his brain that warned this man wasn't the type to stick waved a white flag of surrender, and Chad knew any resistance to the power of this man was futile.

With small movements, Jesse's fingers finally eased in, big, thick, spreading him open. The next shiver lifted his hips and his body took over the begging. When the kisses stopped, Chad opened his eyes to find Jesse looking at him, his expression inscrutable as he carefully slid his fingers out.

"Ready?"

Chad laughed softly. Jesse grinned, and encouraged him to pull a knee up toward his chest. Jesse braced himself with one hand on Chad's leg, then aligned the broad tip of his cock against Chad's opening. The pressure was steady, big, breath-stealing. Then Jesse's gaze dropped as his cock slipped past the tight ring of muscles. He didn't give Chad a chance to catch his breath, just pushed in slow and steady until he was balls-deep.

"Oh. Oh, yes." Chad watched as Jesse's face stilled, and his eyes closed, as if he was struggling to maintain control. That was hot.

Opening his eyes once more, Jesse's mouth curved into a wide smile, flashing his deep laugh lines, and he gave a short, hard thrust of his hips, driving himself deeper. Gripping Chad's hips hard enough to leave bruises, the cowboy set a demanding pace that left no room for questions or second thoughts, no need for promises, no room for anything except their mutual pleasure in the moment. In each other.

****

There weren't many men who could threaten Jesse with a look, but despite the fact he was wearing an apron, Tyler Hardin was making a damn good effort at moving to the top of that list. Given Ty's history as a Navy SEAL and unsure of what he'd done to piss the man off, Jesse figured, it might be good to remind him of their connection. "Nice of you to have me here, Ty. I was sorry to hear about Gibby. Roy's been a friend of mine for a lot of years."

"Is that right? Well, I don't have too many friends, so I take care of the ones I have. So when an old shipmate asks me to keep a watch over his stepson...I take it real personal."

What the fuck? Jesse blinked then took a quick inventory to make sure his mouth wasn't hanging open. "This is a *'What are your intentions?'* talk? Because I got news for you, I don't give a shit what your reputation is—it's none of your goddamn business where I put my dick."

Slipping the narrow band of white cloth over his head, Ty removed his apron and stepped back from the counter. "It is when you're at my place and you take advantage of someone half your age and only an ounce of your experience."

Ouch. That hurt, but Jesse didn't wince. Ty wasn't saying anything he hadn't already told himself a thousand times over. That didn't mean he would back down now. God, it would almost be worth it to take the big man on. Sure he'd get his ass kicked in the end, but it would be interesting to see how long he could stick. Besides, he could use a good fight.

"Get a grip, chef-boy. Chad isn't half my damn age. He's old enough to know what he wants and I gave it to him. No intentions, no roses, and wedding vows. Just a good hard fuck that left us both satisfied." He looked over Ty's shoulder and saw Cass leaning in the dining room doorway, apparently waiting to see what would happen next.

With a tip of an imaginary hat, Jesse gave a quick bow of his head. "Thanks, Cass. Looks like it's time I head for the next rodeo. And, Ty, grow the fuck up. Sometimes a piece of ass is just that—a quick fuck—no strings attached."

With his cowboy swagger on full display, Jesse turned, ready to throw his bag in the truck and hit the damned road. He bit back a curse when he saw Chad standing between him and his exit. *Fuck.*

Well, he'd already stepped in shit up to his elbows...no sense in stopping now. He strode forward and clapped a hand on the smaller man's shoulder, studiously ignoring the over-bright eyes and sexy-as-shit pout. It didn't do a damn bit of good to know he'd put that look of hurt on Chad's face. The best thing for all concerned was for him to follow through on getting the fuck out of there.

"See you around, kid." Letting his words act like a slap in Chad's face, Jesse pushed outside— and didn't let door hit him in the ass.

Chapter Eight

At seven thousand feet, the air in Flagstaff was noticeably thinner than anywhere else in Arizona, but nowhere was it more difficult to breathe than standing in front of the frosted glass door of Child Protective Services. Chad adjusted his tie, straightened his shoulders, then pushed the door open and stepped inside.

The waiting room was empty, sealed off from the interior offices by a second door and a high countered reception desk. As soon as he entered, the glass slid open on the receptionist's window and an older Native American woman looked impassively at him, apparently waiting for him to speak.

"I'm Chad Ollom. I'm here to see Park Williams." He checked his watch, even though he'd looked at the time only moments before he'd stepped inside. *Yep, still twenty after. Please don't make me wait out here...*

"I, uh, have an appointment." His voice rose at the end as if he were asking a question.

The woman continued to stare, and he wondered for a moment if she was hearing impaired or if he'd actually managed to will himself invisible.

"Stop it, Rose," said a disembodied male voice.

A broad grin suddenly split the woman's face and she giggled like a schoolgirl. "I'm just teasing. You know I don't mean anything..."

"Yeah, well cut it out and buzz him in." There was a grating buzzing noise then a distinctive snick as the electronic lock disengaged. Chad pushed through the second door and found himself face-to-face with a man his own age.

"Mr. Ollom? Park Williams. Don't pay Rose any attention, honey. Small mind, small pleasures. Thanks for agreeing to meet with me. It makes things easier. Follow me and we'll head into the conference room."

Trailing behind the other man, Chad took stock of the CPS specialist. Without really knowing what to expect, he could say without hesitation, Park Williams was not...it. Long wavy hair tied back with a blue and gold hair scrunchie, the tail hanging a good six inches below his shoulder. The boxy button front shirt was blazoned with palm trees and Tiki huts, worn untucked. Faded blue jeans rode low on his hips, the legs starting narrow through the thigh then flaring wide in an over-sized boot cut, that looked suspiciously like bell bottoms.

Chad blinked. Gaydar wasn't even remotely necessary, because if the sashaying hips hadn't been signal enough, the thick woolen lavender socks tucked into the neon pink Crocs would have sealed it. Not that he was stereotyping. Well, yeah—he was—but seriously? Pink?

The long narrow hallway extended in both directions, doors open to show small offices, most of them packed with old, over-sized furniture. The predominant decorating theme was stacks of buff-colored file folders. Bypassing the warren of offices in favor of the last doorway at the end of the hall, Park stepped into a conference room that contained an oval oak table two feet too big for the meeting room space. He waved his hand toward the end where it was clear from the folder and pad of paper that he'd been waiting for the meeting to start.

Forcing his feet in a forward motion, Chad was struck by an absurd notion that gravity must have a greater influence at this elevation because his feet weighed roughly the same as a small elephant. Each motion required a conscious, nearly painful effort. Once he was in front of his chair at the table, he risked a look down. The shock of seeing a Child Protective Services folder labeled with his name took the remaining strength from his legs and the breath from his lungs, and Chad collapsed with little grace into the pleather and chrome chair.

"Oh…" he said. His hand shook slightly as he set his backpack on the floor next to his seat. He needed to remain calm, but all he could do was think he was seven times a fool for turning away the WSR attorney after Ty's little display of temper. *Suck it up, Ollom—no going back on that decision now.*

As if he knew what Chad was feeling, Park reached for the folder and flipped it label-side down. "I know it's a shock to find yourself here. I'm a bandage-off-fast sort of person myself, so let's get started."

Chad nodded and watched while Park squeezed into the narrow space between the end of the table and the wall. He kicked off one pink clog and tucked his foot under his butt, then pulled the pad of yellow paper into his lap. It was an absurd position considering the table could seat twelve, but the man seemed to curl into the spot, like a cat.

"Mr. Ollom…look, I feel a bit silly calling you that, considering we're about the same age. Would mind if I call you Chad?"

"No—I don't—" He pressed his fingers to the edge of the table. "Actually, I don't care what you call me. I didn't do anything wrong. The sooner you ask what you need to ask, the better." That was good, he sounded strong. Confident.

Park pressed his lips together, but Chad couldn't tell if he was laughing or angry. He waited.

Park met his gaze, and for a long moment, neither of them spoke. There was nothing confrontational in the look—far from it. It was as if Park weighed Chad's words, and found truth. He nodded once.

"I don't blame you for wanting to get this over with. Let's start with the basics." They spent the next few minutes confirming Chad's identity, current residence, and place of employment. "You should know, part of my duties as an advocate for the child include conducting a thorough investigation," Park said. He tapped the folder on the table and seemed to be choosing his words. "We run background checks on all parties involved whenever there's a report of abuse…"

Chad let the man explain the standard investigation while he worked at building his nerve to ask what had been on his mind since he'd passed through Kingman. It had been such an epiphany that as soon as he'd arrived at the hotel the previous evening, he'd looked at the online version of the CPS Handbook.

"I have a question," Chad interrupted.

Once again Park focused his hazel gaze, and Chad shifted uncomfortably. What if he pissed the man off? Would it hurt his case? Trusting his instincts, Chad forged ahead.

"I really just don't understand. There wasn't any CPS investigation, no formal complaints. Just a few emails and letters from parents, that turned into some sort of witch hunt because I'm gay. I haven't taught anywhere since then...so why now?"

"As I told you on the phone, we had an official complaint to our office. I requested records from all the schools in the county, public and private, where you were listed as a substitute teacher. You are correct in your statement that there was never a formal complaint filed last year, however, you should know, I *did* look into the situation." He put up a hand as Chad started to protest.

"Hang on, let me finish. Our office was under an oversight mandate as a result of another matter entirely. We quite literally had to look at every issue that hinted at possible child abuse in the school district—it wasn't personal—but I did look. At the time, I screened school board meeting minutes, parental support and objection notifications, and your employment records for each location you taught. At that time, the discussion was tabled. If there was further discussion, it was not made part of any official record."

Park lifted the folder and Chad's stomach felt like the Flagstaff pinecone on New Year's Eve, a slow steady drop. This was not going well.

"But I haven't taught anywhere in the county since then." He repeated the words, as if they might make the nightmare go away.

Picking up a fat mechanical pencil, Park opened the folder, ran his finger down the page, and paused. "I need to confirm a few facts. Can you tell me where you were working on September twenty-second last year?"

It was as if the oxygen left the room. Chad felt lightheaded and little spots of light danced in front of his eyes. He inhaled to a count of five, then exhaled just as slowly. Obviously, declining Cass's attorney had been a piss poor idea. Hefting the backpack at his feet into his lap, he rummaged for his datebook. With shaking hands and damp fingers, Chad opened the little book to the month in question. "I was teaching third grade on the Navajo Reservation. I was there all week because the regular teacher broke her ankle."

"At any time on that date did you administer corporal punishment?"

"What? I wouldn't... I never... No." Nerves had prevented him from eating before this meeting, which was a good thing. Nausea roiled in his empty and over-caffeinated stomach. "I taught at that school several times over the last two years. Is that what I'm being accused of? That I hit a child?"

"Did you ever do any substitute work at Mountain View Elementary in Flagstaff?"

Frowning, Chad searched his memory. After a minute, he reached into his bag for an older date book, flipped through some pages. When he found what he was looking for, he looked up. "I never substituted there, but two years ago I completed a one week intern program on integrating art education in the regular classroom. It was supposed to help promote art in the classroom

despite mandated curriculum and budget cuts—"
He took a breath. "Sorry, I get a little passionate
about the need for a well-rounded education..."

Park actually smiled at that as if he knew some
great secret. "No problem. I had a rather
unconventional education, and it included plenty
of art."

For a moment both men smiled at each other.
With a little shake of his head, Park asked Chad to
confirm the dates he'd been at Mountain View.
"Are you certain you've never substituted on the
campus? Never been the sole teacher responsible
for a classroom?"

Genuinely confused, Chad responded with all
sincerity. "Other than that one week, I've never
been on that campus. There were three other
student teachers with me during the internship,
and as far as I can remember, we stayed together
the entire time. Even though we all had our state
fingerprint cards, none of us was left alone on the
campus—I do know that. Can you tell me exactly
what exactly is going on?"

"Hold that thought..." Park untucked his leg,
slipped off the second shoe, and made his way to
the door in his socks. The whole look was beyond
casual, even by Flagstaff standards and Chad
wondered how the man kept his job.

"Janet, can you come in here a minute?" He
padded back to his spot and started to gather his
papers and the folder into a neat stack. He slipped
the Crocs back on his feet, just as a distinguished

woman with silver-streaked hair and tired eyes stepped into the room. Rather than remaining the only one seated, Chad jumped to his feet.

"Janet's the supervisor here," Park said by way of an explanation. "Janet, this is Mr. Chad Ollom. We're all finished. I've completed this part of the investigation, everything is documented. There is no evidence that he had any improper contact with the subject child. In fact, he just confirmed what the independent investigation uncovered. He was not in Flagstaff on the day in question. He has never taught at the school the child attended. He hasn't been on the campus since the subject's family moved to Flag. Oh, and here…" He reached across the table and handed the woman the folders. She frowned at the stack as she tucked it under her arm.

"Shit, Park…" Tears leaked from the corners of the woman's eyes.

Completely off balance, Chad watched a sub-drama play out, feeling as if he'd missed the first twenty minutes of the show.

"Aww, Janet honey. Don't cry. You knew this was coming…" Park retrieved his own backpack from where it had been tucked under his chair. After slinging it over his shoulder, he crossed to the woman and they hugged, murmuring words too softly for Chad to hear. Not that he wanted to know, because he didn't. He just wanted to get the hell out of here, if he was cleared.

Quietly retrieving his date books from the table, Chad put his things back inside his pack. Hanging on by the strap, uncertain if he was free to go, he started to shuffle toward the door.

"I, uh…"

"Hey, Janet, I gotta run, huh? Taco and Scooby are waiting and I want to talk to Chad before he takes off, okay?"

"You better call me," Janet sniffled.

"You know I will. And you have my cell number, in case anything comes up."

"Yeah, sure. That's why your sorry ass is leaving me here at CPS, while you go off to find yourself… Go on. Get out of here before I tie you down and make you stay."

"Promises, promises. Bye, sweetheart. I love you." With a finger wave, Park stepped toward the door, only to retrace his steps and take Chad by the arm. The tug was firm enough to propel him forward, and the man didn't let go until they were all the way outside.

Chad had a million questions, but there was one thing he had to know right now. "Am I done? I mean, no one's going to arrest me or anything?"

"Do you drink coffee?" Park pulled some keys out of his pocket.

"What? Wait, answer my question first." Chad was sure they were running in parallel universes because nothing Park had said in the last fifteen minutes made any sense.

"God, I am seriously caffeine deprived. All I had this morning was instant. Anything else is too hard in the van with Taco and Scooby, since I was already packed and everything. Do you know where Starbucks is on Milton? I'll meet you there."

The man trotted across the lot toward an orange and white VW van that appeared to be rocking off its axles as the dogs inside went wild. "It'll take me a minute, I need to let the boys out first. I'll take a Cinnamon Dolce soy latté. No butter topping. Thirty minutes, tops." With that unhelpful information, he unlocked his van and climbed inside.

****

Standing in line and waiting to order usually just pissed Jesse off, but since this was yet another one of those deals he made with God, Jesse would try to stick to the first part of the bargain, even though God was omnipotent and would have already figured out he'd renege. Just like he usually did. According to his watch, it was just now nine o'clock and Chad was somewhere in Flagstaff for his interview with CPS. Assuming the meeting would take a couple of hours, Jesse gave God the next hour—or one cup of coffee—to help him figure out where the CPS office was and to come up with a plan that didn't sound totally lame.

And if you find him...then what? He hated that fucking little voice in his head. One of God's minions, no doubt.

All right...One cup of coffee. If you can help me figure out how I can find Chad to apologize, I'll uh...give up riding rodeo.

You promised that one last time...

Fine, help me find Chad...and apologize...and make sure he accepts it...and...uhm... I'll settle down.

The woman in front of him in line took half a step forward and glanced nervously over her shoulder when he snorted at his own foolishness. Jesse grinned back at her, probably making her even more uneasy.

Maybe she was right to think he was crazy. Here he was, standing in line for a cup of coffee that he didn't want, arguing with himself, and making deals with God that he had no intention of keeping.

Dismissing the woman and the deal making, Jesse rocked on his feet, trying to loosen the tension in his lower back. He'd stewed all the way to Flagstaff this morning. How the fuck had he not thought to get Chad's cell number? *See ya around, kid.* Could he have been any more condescending? Not that he was interested in anything more than what they'd already done.

For Christ's sake, it wasn't like he'd even been mad at Chad, either. He'd let that fuckin' Ty get under his skin. He'd never meant for Chad to hear that shit. It about killed him to see those damn baby blues peeking out from the shaggy blond hair. He should have taken Chad by the arm and explained he hadn't really meant it the way it sounded.

Oh really? Since when?

"Shut up." When the woman in front of him gasped and looked over her shoulder, Jesse realized he must have spoke that last bit out loud. She shoved her money at the clerk, then scooted around to the other end of the counter.

Jesse ordered his coffee, and since it was just the plain old every day black and straight variety, the boy—he refused to even think the word barista—took his money and handed him the cup, all in one easy step.

Now to find a seat where he could look up the address for CPS and think about what he'd say when Chad came outside and saw him standing there. Because no matter how many deals he'd made with the man upstairs…they always involved his own hard work to make them pay off.

When the door opened, he automatically looked over and nearly sloshed his coffee out of the little hole in the cup lid. *Chad.*

"Oh. Hey, Jesse. What are you doing here?" Chad asked the question, but kept moving toward the counter, forcing Jesse to follow if he wanted to talk.

Chad wore a pair of dark slacks, with pressed creases, a pale blue shirt that matched his eyes, and a navy and gold striped tie. Everything from the neck down was neat, professional, button down sexy. His hair was just as long and untamed as it usually was, and…well, just wild ass sexy. Damn, no matter how you looked, the man was just flat out…sex on wheels.

"Hey, Chad, long time no see," the young man behind the counter said.

"Hey, Rueben. How you doing?" Jesse moved in close behind Chad and placed a hand on his shoulder. *Yeah, it probably looked possessive as hell.*

"I'm good, thanks. You still near Kingman? Looks like you found yourself a cowboy…" Someone behind Jesse cleared his throat and Ruben seemed to realize he needed to keep the line moving. "Sorry, it's good to see you again. What can I get you?"

"A coffee and a Cinnamon Dolce soy latte, please. Hold the butter topping. Oh, and add a couple of muffins, too, please."

"You got it. We'll call your name when it's ready."

Jesse's hand loosely cupped the back of Chad's neck as they moved to the other end of the counter. Fortunately, the woman who'd been eyeing him was long gone. He had some groveling to do and didn't exactly want an audience.

Chad kept his gaze fixed on the workers behind the counter, as they shifted and moved, poured, mixed, and served all while keeping up a happy banter. It reminded Jesse of a bar. A coffee bar…the new place for hook ups?

The thought had him frowning. "A latte? Are you meeting someone?"

Chad shrugged away from the touch and turned to look up at Jesse. "You don't have the right to ask me that."

"Yeah, I deserve that. Look, I didn't know you were behind me. I was reacting to Ty's overbearing parental attitude. And I know that doesn't excuse what I said."

"No, it doesn't, but you didn't say anything that wasn't true. It wasn't his business. And you were absolutely right. Sometimes a fuck is just a fuck. We had a good one—no strings attached."

"Order is ready for Chad," a young woman called out.

Jesse stood back and watched as Chad gathered up his breakfast, then without looking his way again, pushed outside and set the items on a table near the back corner of the small patio.

Jesse frowned as it became clear Chad wasn't going to offer an invitation to join him. He wanted to ask Chad about his interview. He wanted to explain more about what had happened at the ranch, and maybe even about the deal he made a few minutes ago. Chad was acting as if they barely knew each other.

You dumb jackass. When have you ever bothered to get know any of the quick fucks? Realizing he was in danger of sinking back into an unwinnable argument with himself, Jesse grabbed a newspaper and tourist map, then pushed through the door and took a seat at a table cattycorner from where Chad waited for his...date?

Idly, he watched a vintage VW bus pull into the lot and park. With a great deal of hand waving and finger shaking, the man was clearly issuing orders and trying to maintain some sense of control as he worked at exiting his van. He almost made it, too. Almost. Then there was madcap barking, and he tumbled out the door in a jumble of leashes, long hair, bellbottoms, and hideous pink shoes. Smothering a laugh, Jesse was up and crossing the lot before he could think about what he was doing. A speeding bullet in the guise of a pint-sized Chihuahua broke free and raced toward the busy Route 66 traffic. Jesse dove left and rolled with his fall, catching the looped handle of the leash with one finger. The dog was air-bound as his momentum carried him forward until his leash ran out of slack and he crashed to the ground with a strangled yelp.

Lying on his back, sucking in air, Jesse blinked up at the little dog who now stood trembling...not with fear, but with apparent rage. He might have laughed if there had been any breath left in his lungs. The dragon wannabe's growl was bigger than he was.

Squeezing in a breath past the spasms in his side from the still slightly bruised ribs, Jesse spoke quietly. He'd always had a way with animals. "Hey there, pup, it's okay. I got you." The little dog straightened his forelegs and the growl turned into a high-pitched yap-yap-yap.

"Scooby! Scooby, you stop that right now! That nice man just saved your life." The longhaired hippy type was standing over him and reaching for the leash. "I am so sorry. Hand me his leash and I'll help you up."

"Scooby? Seriously?" He handed over the leash but only allowed himself to come up as far as a sitting position. With his arms folded over his bent knees Jesse stayed on the ground. He needed to sit and catch his breath before he tackled standing.

"Yup, this here Scooby. The big guy over there is Taco."

Chad had moved over toward the van and was holding on to the collar of the biggest dog Jesse had ever seen in person. The damn thing looked like an escapee from the pony ride at the fair. And seeing Chad standing there, looking like this hippy was his date really pissed Jesse off. He looked back up at the outstretched hand.

"A Chihuahua and a Great Dane. Nice. And you even come with your own van. Do your friends call you Shaggy, too?"

The man grinned down at him and flicked his hair over his shoulder. "The name's Park, but as long as you don't call me by your last boyfriend's name, you can call me anything—or anytime—you want to."

Jesse snorted back a laugh. This time, he accepted the offer of a hand and pushed himself to his feet. With a hiss, he felt around his bruised ribcage. Looked like any plans to catch up to the rodeo had just been derailed for another couple of weeks. Just as well, considering his conversation with Cass just before he'd left the ranch. Coming fully upright, Jesse smashed his hat onto his head, then brushed at the seat and tugged at the crotch of his jeans.

"Well hellooo, cowboy. Gotta horse you need me to save?"

Jesse rolled his eyes. "Nice to meet you, Park. Good luck with your beast." He nodded at Scooby, turned to Chad, but dropped his gaze and muttered, "Taco."

Fifteen years on the rodeo circuit taught you there were just times it was better to walk away while you still could. It was a lesson Jesse mostly sucked at because the minute someone said he couldn't...or shouldn't, well...it was like a damn aphrodisiac. But after spending a couple of days at the WSR, Jesse realized he was tired. It went bone deep. And after all, a deal was a deal.

"Hey, cowboy? You look a little shook up. Maybe you shouldn't be driving quite yet. Let me buy you a cup of coffee for saving my dog and you can come sit over here with us for just a little while before you leave. No hurry, right? What's your name?"

"Jesse. Jesse Duran meet Park Williams." Chad stepped forward, hand now tucked firmly into Taco's leash.

"Oh, hey! I didn't realize you two were friends. Chad, you can bring Taco right there on to the patio. You guys have a seat and wait for me. What do you drink , Jesse?"

"Coffee. Thanks, just black."

When Park finally returned, he handed Jesse the coffee then fell into his seat and dramatically grabbed his own latte. He swallowed down half of the sweet drink before he finally stopped to take a breath. "Well that was a heck of a way to enter my next phase of retirement."

"So this really is your last day with CPS?" Chad handed over the leash then took a sip of his own coffee.

"Yes. It was supposed to be yesterday, but I wanted to finish out your part of this case..." Park's gaze flicked to Jesse for a moment before settling back on Chad. His mouth formed a thin line as if he pressed it tight to keep from saying anything he shouldn't.

"It's okay. Jesse knows why I'm here. Or at least he knows why I came to Flagstaff. Maybe you could tell us both why I'm here meeting with you?"

"Simple." Park reached into his shoulder bag and whipped out a compact and used the little applicator pad. "Someone is trying to frame your ass. I thought you should know." With that startling pronouncement, Park began to dust a fine layer of powder over his cheeks and nose.

Chad's eyebrows rose in obvious amusement. "Frame me? For what? Why would anyone want to frame me? I did exactly what the homophobes wanted. I left town—I didn't fight for my job. They won."

Digging into his bag once more, Park came out with a slender pencil. Jesse watched in a sort of horrified fascination as with a steady hand and only an occasional glance in the mirror, he drew a line along the upper and lower lashes. Licking his pinkie finger, Park smudged the upper line at the base of his lashes. "Honey, I don't have any idea why—that's up to you to figure out. I just thought you should know."

Chapter Nine

Chad opened the door to the ranch truck and climbed heavily from the cab. The buildings were mostly dark, with only an occasional lighted window breaking the plane of darkness to indicate someone inside was still awake. With his backpack hanging from one shoulder, he trudged across the darkened yard toward his house, more tired than he'd thought possible. Not so much from the long day, but from all the emotional upheaval of the last forty-eight hours. He wished it could all be dismissed as OPD, Other People's Drama, but unfortunately, it had all belonged to him. The good news was, it might soon be over. At least the biggest hurdle was crossed. From what Park had explained this morning, there was nothing linking Chad to any further investigation. He was cleared. Period. That relief was overwhelming.

After Park relayed the news that Chad was in the clear, Jesse had stood, done that stupid tip of the hat trick, then sauntered off to his truck. With a quick firing of the diesel engine, the big cowboy had driven out of his life. Which was better for everybody. Really. Because who knew what words Chad might have said if Jesse had stuck around. Had held him. Had even once hugged him and said everything would be okay...

Rubbing at the center of his chest, Chad opened the door to his casita. As soon as the door was closed, his fingers loosened the death grip he had on the strap of his backpack, and the heavy bag thudded to the floor. With a sigh, he fell back against the door and dropped his head, letting the familiar smell of home wash over him.

"You made it home. Everything okay?"

Chad jumped, slamming his head back against the door, fight or flight instincts on full alert. "Jesse?"

Of course it was Jesse. Who else would think it was okay to sneak into his house in the middle of the night and scare him half to death. And never mind that Jesse hadn't been sneaking—lurking in the dark was just as bad. He let the adrenaline drive his anger, fed it with hurt, and layered on resentment.

"Yes, I made it—thank you for stating the obvious. What the fuck are you doing in my house?" Chad flipped on the light switch as he spoke and barely kept enough breath to finish his sentence.

The sleeping bag had been unzipped and spread open on the couch. And so was Jesse. All six-foot-something, narrow hipped, broad shouldered, naked bit of him. Unwrapped like Christmas morning and looking deliciously, sleepily rumpled. It wasn't goddamn fair.

Jesse blinked, rubbed his eyes, then smothered a yawn. In a voice that scratched at every one of Chad's itches, he said, "Was waiting for you. Musta fallen asleep."

Naked and waiting for him with a slow, easy smile. As if that somehow made everything okay.

Years before, Chad had been completing his application for postgraduate school and had to describe a personal strength he brought to the classroom. The answer had come easily: an even-tempered ability to maintain control, regardless of the provocation. Right now, Jesse was sorely testing that temper, but Chad wasn't about to let the smug cowboy use that sleepy smile to worm back into his good graces.

Ignoring his rising blood pressure, Chad narrowed his eyes and leveled a look that had been known to strike fear in the hearts of fourth graders. The look could quell a room of thirty children, turn unsuspecting parents into field trip chaperones, and was guaranteed to stop a running child in his tracks.

Jesse's lips twitched, and the lines around his eyes fanned into deep creases. Then he coughed, cleared his throat, and tried to pretend it hadn't been laughter. "Come here, Chad." He sat up and patted the couch next to him.

The tiredness he'd fought all the way home washed over Chad and he sank heavily against the door and rubbed at the back of his neck. When he asked again, there was no heat to the words, just a weary acceptance that for whatever reason, the cowboy wasn't ready to make himself scarce, yet. They seemed to go back and forth, like a bad game of tag. He really shouldn't be feeling a slow spread of warmth through his chest at that thought. He tried to toughen his resolve, but what was the point. He knew where this was headed. "Goddamn you, Jesse. Why are you here? What do you want?"

****

Why am I here? Good fucking question.

"I told you, I wanted to apologize."

"You did that, already. In Flagstaff, remember?"

Jesse closed his eyes for a moment and rubbed the back of his neck. This wasn't exactly going how he'd hoped it would.

Oh, what? You thought you'd lay here all naked and Chad would walk in and climb on?

"Something like that."

"Something like what?" Chad asked. Jesse realized he'd spoken aloud. That miniature version of Jiminy Cricket running around in his head was too much. He was either going crazy or spending way too much time alone.

"Sorry…just…thinking…. Look, Chad…" he stopped. Other than his truck and saddle, he didn't have anything he called his own. A guy like Chad probably couldn't understand. Sure he'd had a bad time with his real dad when he was a kid. But obviously his mom must have married a good guy, since his stepdad had Ty ready to do battle on his behalf. Jesse cleared his throat. Decided to try something else.

"Uhm, what did Park say after I left? Is there really any evidence someone framed you?"

"I think Park likes his drama, but yes, this seemed above and beyond a typical case of a homophobic parent's complaint. You didn't have to leave, you know. It wasn't like Park was allowed to give me a lot of details."

"I…uh…" Jesse shook his head and blew out a breath. Tried again. Something about those baby blues and shaggy blond hair just got to him. He needed to make sure Chad knew exactly what he was in for with a guy like him.

"Look, Chad. I've been on the rodeo circuit as a pro since I was seventeen. That's nearly twenty years of going from show to show, riding other people's horses, making my living eight seconds at a time. Anything longer than that…I don't stick."

"I think I get that. So, for the third time tonight…why are you here, Jesse?"

"Fuck if I know."

Chad barked a laugh. "You can do better than that, cowboy."

Jesse stood, and when Chad's smile didn't falter, he closed the distance between them. "Maybe"—he leaned down and licked at Chad's lips—"I'm not finished with you yet."

"More like I'm not finished with you. I'm under your skin, Jesse Duran, and that scares the hell out you."

"Shut the fuck up and get naked." He didn't recognize the deep growl of his own voice, but as his erection bumped high on Chad's stomach, there was no denying his body's reaction to the other man's words. *Not finished with me.*

While Chad kicked off his shoes and unfastened his pants, Jesse worked the buttons on the dress shirt. "Liked the tie, earlier…where is it?"

Chad let his pants drop to the floor. "Took it off in the truck." He traced his hand over Jesse's chest, lingering for a moment on the faded crease of a scar on his left pec. "I kind of like the look of you naked. There's a story, here."

"Steamboat Springs. 2005, I think. Happened on the first ride of the rodeo. My hand slipped in the glove, the bronc went left, and I didn't. Missed the rest of the weekend."

Chad didn't say anything, just moved his hand to the next scar, a wicked looking pink crescent on his shoulder.

"Yeah, that one hurt. 2010, Williams, Arizona. Made it to the final round, then drew a for-shit horse. Motherfucker tossed every single cowboy that weekend. It was the final round and I was his last rider, so he put on a show. Stomped on me for good measure." Chad leaned forward and traced the scar with his tongue before leaving it with a gentle kiss. Still not speaking, he licked and kissed his way to Jesse's left collarbone. It was getting hard to remember the details of the damn scars. Chad's mouth was hot and pushing all of his damn buttons.

"Las Cruces. Uhm...Jesus." Chad's teeth scraped against the ridge of scar tissue, then he nibbled his way across and sucked at the base of Jesse's neck. This was nothing like what he was used to. Sex was quick. Hard. Convenient. Get on and get off before anybody got hurt.

"Come on, Jesse. Let's take this into the bathroom, I could use a shower. Maybe we'll find some more places to kiss and make better."

Jesse knew he was grinning like a fool. With a nudge, he encouraged Chad to step in front and lead the way. He let out a long, low whistle. "Damn, baby...I had it right all along. That is one damn beautiful butt."

Chad's laugh was husky, and he added a little extra swivel as he led the way to his bedroom and the master bath.

As soon as they entered the bathroom, Jesse looked around appreciatively. "I love this bathroom—whoever designed this place knew what he was doing. An over-sized shower and a whirlpool tub? I can't even begin to tell you how many times I could have used that at the end of a hard day."

"Thanks—"

"Did you—" Jesse reached into the shower and adjusted the water so that the three spray heads were right where he wanted them. He looked over his shoulder and tracked Chad's movements in the mirror. "Did you—build this place?" he finished the full question. *Why in the hell am I making small talk?*

"Yeah. Well, sort of. I started with the plans from the other two casitas, but Cass pretty much gave me free rein once he realized I knew what I was doing." Chad opened the medicine cabinet and removed a couple of condom packets and a bottle of lube. He pulled two rolled towels out of a wicker basket in the corner and draped them over hooks outside the glass shower door.

Jesse decided he'd been patient enough. With a hand on Chad's bicep and a growl in his throat, he pulled the smaller man inside and put him under the steaming spray. First item on the agenda? Kissing them both senseless. Chad moved into him, melting against Jesse, their skin and their tongues sliding together.

Chad's blond locks darkened as the water spilled over his head. He reached blindly for the shelf that contained his shampoo, and Jesse realized the man really did want a shower before they did anything else. Taking the bottle, Jesse poured the citrus scented shampoo into the palm of his hand, then massaged it into Chad's long hair.

The sexy moan had his cock leaking, and he wished he'd gloved up before they got started. Directing the spray higher, he rinsed until the suds slid away then turned Chad to face him. Jesse sank to his knees, anxious for his first real taste of the other man. They both groaned as he wrapped his lips around the broad cap, his tongue lapping at the salty pre-cum.

With the spill of water creating a curtain around them, Jesse slid Chad's cock into his mouth, then withdrew, the suction sharp, hungry. Faster and faster he went, gripping Chad's hips, a driving rhythm that had the other man thrusting deep into his mouth. Chad's thighs trembled, and his balls drew up, and Jesse was torn by twin desires. As much as he wanted to swallow Chad down, he had been holding onto his fantasy for days. He pulled off with a pop, causing poor Chad to groan and his knees wobble.

"Fuck, Jesse."

"That's the idea. Can't get the first night out of my head…in the barn. Want you to ride my cock like that."

"Oh, hell yes…hand me the lube." Chad propped a foot on the tile bench seat that ran along the back of the shower and started prepping his own hole.

Jesse wanted to fall down and worship at the man's feet—he was so fucking hot that only the water on his back was preventing spontaneous combustion. He wanted that strong, hot body wrapped around him, holding him, surrounding him. He might just shoot watching those slick fingers slide in and out of the pretty pink pucker. Pushing to his feet, Jesse's hands trembled slightly as he tore open the foil packet, and rolled the condom over his straining cock.

"Ready? I want your legs around my waist."

Glazed eyes looked up at him, kiss-swollen mouth slightly open, breath as ragged as his own. Then Chad reached for him, kept one foot on the bench and with a surprisingly swift movement, hopped straight onto Jesse. Wrapping his arms around the wet, slippery body, Jesse shifted his feet to find his center of gravity. Then again, he'd been off balance practically from the minute they'd met. No one had ever pushed his buttons the way Chad could.

"Shit, gonna fall, Jesse."

"I got you." Jesse leaned further back against the wall, bending his knees slightly, angling his hips forward. Grabbing a handful of that magnificent ass, Jesse used his other hand to align his cock before he pressed his way into the silky hot channel.

Chad inhaled on a hiss. Jesse froze. The last thing he wanted to do was hurt the younger man. He should have waited, tried this later when they'd had more time to prep.

"Shit, sorry. Did I hurt you?"

"Big this way."

"Fucking tight this way, too." Jesse raised Chad's hips and started to withdraw.

"No, wait. Just—give me a second." Shifting his grip from holding his own prick, Jesse started to stroke Chad's back, then remembered the rough state of his hands. Changing directions, he threaded his fingers into the long, wet hair, and mashed their mouths together.

When Chad started to push down on him, Jesse pulled back to murmur, "Easy, s'okay..." He'd stared to say they could wait, they could move to the bed, they could suck each other off. Except each phrase floated away on a shot of pleasure as Chad kept pressing steadily downward as his hole swallowed up Jesse's dick. With a moan, Jesse fell back against the cool tile, tilted his hips forward, and kept his hands clamped on Chad, keeping his lover tight against his body.

In this position, they were face to face, and Chad's beautiful blue eyes seemed to widen with each inch gained until Jesse was fully seated in his lover's channel. "Don't...can't...stop. S' soooo hot." Then he pulled up and plunged down again. And again. Using every muscle he had, Jesse pressed hard against the wall for balance, gripped Chad's ass and the back of his head and held tight while the smaller man took him on the ride of his life.

When the channel surrounding his cock began to spasm and Chad's hips lost their rhythm, Jesse pushed a hand between their slippery bodies to capture the hot splash of cum mingled with the water trailing down their bodies. His whole body tensed and he shot so hard he thought Chad might damn well get bucked clear of his ride.

When they were finished, Chad rested his forehead against Jesse's, and reached around to turn off the shower, as the hot water waned. Jesse trembled from head to foot as if he'd been busting a bull in the final round of the national championships. Giving in to gravity at last, Jesse's feet started to slide, until he landed on the bottom of the stall with a slap of wet skin and a lap full of Chad. Jesse sat there with Chad cradled in his arms, pressed tight to his chest, both of them breathing hard. When Chad looked up, those big eyes seemed to see straight into Jesse's soul. He knew what the other man wanted to hear, knew deep down he'd felt more alive in his few days with Chad than he'd ever felt before. The way they just seemed to fit together, not just sex, but everywhere. God, he'd laughed more in the time he'd known Chad than he'd laughed in years.

Chad, the ranch, closing out his career...this made it all seem easy. Too easy. Giving those three little words away? Yeah, that was easy, too— A hell of a lot easier than they were to live up to and he just...couldn't do it. Not now.

"Don't worry about it, cowboy. I think I'm falling fast enough for both of us."

Chapter Ten

T-bone spent a few minutes not moving, just watching Tanner through the binoculars. His brother had chosen well. Tanner lay on his stomach, perched next to a large rocky outcropping, camouflaged in khaki and drab green. Although the WSR's landscape wasn't as heavily wooded as the eastern side of the Trip-T, there were still plenty of pinion and junipers mixed in with the scrub oaks and manzanitas. A man on foot could stay hidden, if he was good. Or careful. T-bone considered himself both. Still, he might not have spotted Tanner if he hadn't been following him for the three hours. Watching. Waiting.

Tanner's binoculars were trained on a horse and rider in the distance, a rider following the game trail, heading inexorably toward the narrow pass below his brother's hiding place. The rifle on the rocks next to Tanner showed his intentions. As if he'd heard T-bone's thoughts, Tanner set the binoculars aside and picked up the rifle, tracking his would-be victim with the scope. For just a minute, T-bone thought about staying where he was and waiting to see what would happen. Taking a firmer grip on the handle of the sawed off baseball bat, he moved off once again, tracking quietly through the brush, closing the steady distance he'd maintained. Tanner would choke. Or worse. It was that *'or worse'* scenario that caused T-bone to quicken his step.

As was typical in the desert in the spring, there was a steady wind, with occasional gusts that kept the trees moving and the dust blowing. Tanner was focused on the horizon, on the scant quarter mile distance separating him and his target. No way would he hear someone at his backside until it was too late. The tension in his brother's body became evident as T-bone moved in. His head was still, shoulders hunched up close to his ears, while he stared through the scope. The hand bracing the forestock appeared steady, but his finger tapped against the trigger guard.

With less than ten feet between them, Tanner suddenly moved. At first T-bone thought the sudden shift was because his brother had heard his approach. Then Tanner let the rifle drop from his hands and he sat up. With jerky movements, he pulled his shirt over his head and tossed it aside. Next came the undershirt. Grabbing his rifle and he started to tie the white T-shirt to the barrel of the rifle.

Oh fuck! The bastard was going to surrender. He would show himself and reveal all of the general's plans to the enemy. *Fuck that!*

With Tanner's attention divided between the rider and his impromptu flag making, he never even turned around as T-bone closed the last few feet, the bat already moving. The solid thud reverberated up his arm, jarring his elbow and leaving his wrist stinging.

The rest of the little drama was like a perfectly choreographed dance. T-bone was in charge and his partners would follow his lead. He gave Tanner a few more blows then stomped down on his ankle, just to make sure he stayed put. If necessary, he could return to his brother once he'd taken care of the approaching rider. He didn't need to kill either man, outright. Just incapacitate them both with serious injuries. Given the coyotes and scavenger birds in the area, the two men would be dead before sunrise, tomorrow. And if by chance the bodies were ever discovered, the pattern of bone breaks would make it look as if they'd beaten each other half to death and nature had taken care of the rest.

With a quick yank, Tim tore his shirt before grabbing a handful of dirt and rubbing it on his face and clothes. That should be just enough. It wasn't like he needed a disguise, just a lure. None of the witnesses would live long enough to remember he'd even been here.

****

With a gentle message of his knees, Jesse turned Angel to the east. Cass had seemed surprised to see him this morning, but when he told the ranch owner he needed a nice quiet place to think and wanted to be productive while he was doing it, Cass had seemed to understand. Maybe they had more in common than he'd first thought. Thinking of the big cowboy with his Navy cook made Jesse smile. He imagined meeting Ty and falling in love had been like a thunderbolt, raising the electricity in the air around Cass and smacking him in the forehead with a bang. He knew the feeling.

Not that Jesse was in love with Chad. He couldn't be. First of all, they'd just met. So—attraction? Sure. Lust? No doubt. But love? Jesse shook his head as the thoughts from the night tried to make themselves heard. This was harsh reality of broad daylight. The time for dreaming was over.

Chad was everything Jesse wasn't. College educated—a teacher, no less and still taking classes online. Jesse hadn't even finished high school. Chad had family and friends who looked out for him. Jesse had been on his own since he was fifteen and on the road a year after that. He'd worked odd jobs and followed the rodeo and life suited him well. Then the inner devil's advocate was on him in a flash.

You are thirty-seven years old. Even the doc said your body wasn't going to hold out at this pace much longer. You gonna be a fucking rodeo clown when you retire from competition?

Okay, so maybe it was time to be serious about settling down. He owed Cass three more weeks of work, minimum. Plus there had been talk about expanding the cutter program. Spending his days training working horses, keeping an eye on the breeding, bringing rough stock to the occasional rodeo...he grinned at the fantasy. That might have been taking Cass's proposal a little too far. Still, the idea was starting to form and the thought of settling down to do that type of work wasn't nearly as suffocating as it had been a year ago.

I'm under your skin, Jesse Duran...I'm falling fast enough for both of us...

Despite the growing heat of the day, Jesse shivered at the memory of those words. It was hard to say which comment was working it's way through his defenses the fastest. Spitting the dust from his mouth, Jesse took the water bottle from the front pack and pulled a long drink. Retirement was a closer reality than ever before, but that didn't mean it had to be at the WSR. It was a nice enough place and maybe he would seriously think about staying if it hadn't been for Chad. But the young man changed the playing field by imagining he was falling in love. Jesse was far too old to let Chad limit himself to someone like him.

Thoughts continued to circle in his brain as he and Angel made their way toward the fence line he would be inspecting today. And if it happened to take him past the spot where he and Chad first made love—so be it. He could admit to himself that had been the plan, Chad would never have to know.

As he looked around the beautiful chaparral vegetation and thought about settling down, Jesse knew this was just the type of place he'd like have when it came time. The right elevation, moderate climate, rocks, trees, and miles of blue sky in every direction. He had very few expenses and other than those associated with his truck and travel. Between his prize money and odd jobs, Jesse had enough to buy himself a small plot of land. He just needed to figure out how he was going to make enough money to build someplace to live. Until then? Well, he'd slept in the bed of his truck before.

A low moan and slight rustle of the brush caught his attention and had Angel skittering in surprise. Reining in his horse, Jesse held his breath as he listened for the sound again. Another small snap of dried brush and quiet groan had him dismounting. Jesse pulled his rifle from the saddle holster. Even without all the shit that had been going on at the ranch lately, there was always the danger of rattlesnakes—no one rode the range without being armed.

Getting his bearings, Jesse scanned the area for any signs of life. There was no movement, no hint of anything out of place. It had been a man's voice, he was sure of that. He couldn't see any sign of a horse, but the only thing that made sense was one of the men who'd ridden out at dawn had some kind of accident and lost his mount. He hadn't seen any sign of a loose horse heading back for the barn, and although a well-trained ranch horse might stay by his rider, he didn't see anyone. Either way whoever was down needed his help.

"Hello? Are you hurt?" Jesse kept his voice soft, not wanting to spook any horses that might be hidden from view. It would carry far enough in the quiet.

"Thank God, someone found us. Hang on, Tanner...hang on." The voice was panicky, urgent. "Hey, we're over here." A man in a torn shirt, looking worse for wear emerged from between densely growing junipers atop a steep cliff face. It wasn't particularly high, but Jesse couldn't see an easy path to reach the top.

"Hold on, I've got to find a path up. Is everyone okay?"

"Be careful, there's a game trail just to the south side."

"Got it, I'm heading up. Why don't you tell me what happened?"

"Rattler. My brother's horse panicked. I tried to grab him—I did!" The stranger's voice rose to a panicked whine that made Angel snort.

"Hey, it's okay, but I need you to stay calm." Jesse divided his attention between the narrow crevice he was climbing and searching for rattlers. If the brothers had seen one, there were likely others in the vicinity.

It was hard to say what happened. One hand clung tight to the trunk of a small oak, while he used the rifle butt in the other hand to push forward. With a shower of pebbles and stones, the rock shelf he'd been standing on gave way. Jesse dove forward, trying to propel himself up one more step. From the corner of his eye he had a glimpse of something moving toward his head with a blinding swiftness. For just a moment, it seemed as if everything slowed down and he could feel every beat of his heart, every labored breath.

Caught between a rock and a hard place, his inner voice mocked.

Suspended in midair, even as he tried to jerk out of the way of the home run swing aimed at his head, Jesse had final moment of clarity. He'd walked straight into a trap. *Fuck*. Then the side of his head exploded.

Chapter Eleven

"Thanks for taking the time with the investigator and the insurance adjuster this morning, Chad. I had them set up to meet with you tomorrow, since I didn't actually expect to see you today."

Chad looked at Cass's tired eyes and regretted his momentary resentment of the delay.

"No worries, Cass. I've got nowhere to go, and until they settle this thing with the fire, I've got nothing to do. Anyplace you want me to be working?"

Cass narrowed his eyes and looked at him for a long minute. "Come to think of it, I actually didn't expect to see Jesse this morning, either. And there he was, sauntering up to the kitchen about thirty minutes after I handed out assignments. He was looking for something to keep himself busy. Wonder why that is?"

Chad turned away, stared toward the distant hills, and bit at the inside of his lips.

"There was a time when I thought all I needed was this ranch, all these wide open spaces, big sky. A man can breathe out here, can feel things without actually having to talk about them. Your horse doesn't give a good goddamn if you go three hours without saying a word."

The big cowboy walked slowly toward the paddock and Chad followed along, curious as to where this story was going. When they reached the split rail fence, Cass pushed his cowboy hat so it sat farther back on his head and leaned his elbows on the top log.

"Do you know the story of Tyler's arrival on the ranch?"

Chad shook his head.

"Before Ty, I was a whole lot like Jesse. Oh sure, I had a working ranch, but deep inside, I was completely content to be that lone cowboy. Go where I wanted to go"—he winced—"do who I wanted to do. And then..." He shrugged. There was a long pause, and Chad wondered if that was all the tall cowboy planned to say. Then Cass cleared his throat and continued. "Settling down was the furthest thing from my mind. But practically from the moment I saw him, resisting Ty was like trying to hold on to my hat in a hurricane. I didn't stand a damn chance. Didn't mean I didn't try to fight it, though." Cass thumped his chest. "In here...I was like Jesse. Self-sufficient, cruising through life, alone without ever recognizing I was lonely."

"I don't think—"

"I gathered from Jesse that everything worked out okay in Flagstaff yesterday." Cass cut him off. "This isn't any of my business, we all know Ty was out of line the other morning. But I'm going to ask you now, Chad. Assuming Jesse sticks around to work a few more weeks, do you want him to stay in your casita?"

Chad turned his head and stared at his small house, as if the structure contained the answer. "Why did Jesse come to Flagstaff yesterday?"

"Didn't you ask him?"

"We, uhm...didn't get to talk much."

Cass threw his head back and laughed and Chad smiled in response.

"Ty chews his ass for besmirching your virtue and goads him into saying shit to you he doesn't mean. An hour later you're gone to Flag and Jesse's in my office apologizing for leaving the ranch short-handed and asking if I mind if he sticks around." Cass dropped a heavy arm onto Chad's shoulders. "The next thing I know, he asks for the day off. What the fuck do you think he was doing in Flagstaff?"

"He was looking for me?"

Shrugging, Cass gazed toward the trail Jesse took earlier. His eyes narrowed and he straightened to his full height.

"What the… Fuck."

Chad followed his gaze and saw Angel trotting toward the barn, but Jesse was nowhere in sight.

"Shit," Chad said, pushing his fear of the animal aside to move forward and try to draw the horse to him. If he could only catch the reins. He just knew something was seriously wrong for Angel to come back riderless. Vaguely aware of Cass raising the alarm and the shouts of men as they raced to get mounts from the barn, Chad kept his attention focused, held his hand out in the most non-threatening manner, and called softly to the horse.

"Come, Angel. Here, boy, where's Jesse?" God, the horse would never forgive him for talking to him like he was a dog. Angel came to a halt, just beyond Chad's outstretched arm. Running his hand over the horse's neck, Chad looked for any sign the horse—or his rider—had been hurt. Seeing nothing, Chad gathered the reins in one hand and stood on his toes in order to reach his foot into the stirrups. Not giving himself time for second thoughts, Chad pushed up, swung his leg over, foot searching for the other stirrup. Shit, they were too long, but as if conveying his own sense of urgency, Angel had already turned and was now retracing the trail.

With an awareness of living his nightmare, Chad clutched at the saddle horn and dug with his feet until he'd hooked both into the looped leather that held the stirrups. Not quite as secure, but better than letting his legs flop against the horse's flanks. Chad prayed the horse knew where he was going, because he sure as shit wasn't any more in charge of this ride than he'd been in charge of Rajun' when he'd been eight years old. Thirteen years earlier, the ride had cost him everything he'd believed in...he couldn't lose it all again. Jesse had to be all right.

When Angel finally started to slow down, Chad risked letting go of the saddle with one hand, long enough to stroke the sweaty black neck.

"Is this it? Are we here, big guy?" Chad looked around and thought the scenery looked vaguely familiar, as they were near the place he and Jesse made love. Angel came to a full stop and Chad slid from the saddle on shaky legs and looked around.

"You better not be fucking with me—" Chad continued to mutter to the horse under his breath, but something told him the horse had brought him here for a reason.

The terrain was particularly rugged in this narrow passage. People unfamiliar with the west assumed a working ranch would have large grassy fields where the cattle munched themselves into a stupor. Chad had been at the WSR long enough to know the cattle per acre ratio was much different than in other parts of the country. Arizona was still mostly an open range state; cows roamed free through hundreds of acres of land, eating rangeland grasses supplemented by feed. So recent signs of cattle passing through were evident even in the rocky hills and the most remote ranch locations like one.

The trail split in two very different directions. He would have to hazard a guess as to which way Jesse might have gone if he couldn't find him here. One part of the trail looped back, and he thought if he remembered the maps, it would eventually lead back to the main part of the ranch. The other was a very narrow game trail that ran up the south side of a twenty-foot sheer rock wall. If Jesse had been going any further east he would have passed through that narrow opening. With a sick feeling growing in the pit of his stomach, Chad hurried forward, sure this was where he was supposed to look. It didn't take long. Once he cleared the dense stand of manzanita, he caught sight of familiar worn boots.

"Oh, fuck. Jesse!"

The ground where Jesse lay was littered with sharp shards of quartz, larger chunks of granite, sandstone and surrounded by juniper trees. Blood seeped into the ground around his head. Although he was lying on his back, there was a large wound at his temple. Chad reached with trembling fingers and found a pulse. *Jesus.*

Recalling his first aid knowledge, Chad knew the most important thing he could do was get help first. Since Jesse's cell phone was still attached to his pocket, Chad unclipped it, thumbed through the speed dial numbers, and called Cass.

"I've got him, Cass. He's hurt—could be bad. He's unconscious, and the side of his head is bloody. Just follow the trail and go east from where I left Angel."

"Okay, no worries, we're right behind you, Chad. Others are on their way. Make sure the area is safe for you—no snakes or anything, and then give first aid. Hang on..." There were murmured voices in the background. "Bryan says to stop any bleeding first, but don't try to move him. We can't be that far behind you—maybe five minutes at the outside. Just keep the line open, we'll be right there."

Relieved that Bryan—former Navy corpsman—was with Cass, Chad confirmed Jesse wasn't bleeding anywhere, other than the slow ooze from the wound on his head.

Kneeling next to Jesse's head he gently brushed at the dirt on the big man's face. There were several scratches on his cheekbone and more visible through his shadow beard. Glancing at the wall of rock, Chad tried to make out what happened. Near as he could tell, Jesse might not even have been on Angel's back when he'd fallen. What could he possibly have been looking at on top of that steep hill?

"Hey…that you, BB?" Chad's attention snapped back down and he was relieved to see Jesse looking back. Maybe the gaze was a little unfocused, but thank God, Jesse's eyes were open and he clearly recognized Chad.

"Hey, cowboy. You gave me a scare. Stay still, help is coming." He stroked his fingers over the uninjured patches of skin.

"Help?" His voice sounded as if he'd swallowed some of the same dirt he was wearing. "What happened? Was there an accident?"

Deciding against offering a drink until Bryan gave the okay, Chad focused on keeping him talking.

"That's the question of the day. Did you fall off Angel?"

"Angel?" His gaze wandered to the cliff and back. "I don't think so. What happened?" He repeated his question and moved his hands as if he was thinking about pushing himself up.

Chad placed his hand in the middle of Jesse's chest, a gentle pressure keeping him in place. "We don't know what happened, Jesse. Bryan and Cass are on their way here." Jesse's brow furrowed, so Chad provided little more information. "Remember Cass? This is his ranch. Bryan's got the medical training."

"I remember…shit. I remember you said…"

"Yeah, well. You don't need to worry about what I said. I won't say it again, okay? You just stay still, though, I don't want you to hurt something in there permanently." He could hear Cass and Bryan dismounting near where he'd left Angel. "We're over here," he called out.

Jesse reached up to touch his head, but again Chad stopped him. "You just stay still. I think you need an ambulance or maybe it's medevac helicopter out here, right?"

"Will you stop fussing? You're starting to act like a damn rodeo doctor. Help me sit up—"

"You work for me, right now, Jesse Duran, and I say you stay put until Bryan here can check you out." Cass's gravel voice growled out as he and Bryan approached.

Chad rose, and moved back to stand next to Cass while Bryan crouched down at Jesse's side. They watched for moment and then as if by common consent they turned and began to look around the area for signs of what might've happened. Cass found the spot where the narrow passage between the rocks had given way and tumbled into a miniature avalanche.

With a slight frown, Cass started to clear the trail, as if he was going to climb to the top of the steep hill.

"Hey, Cass? What's the easiest access if we want to get him into town and checked out? I think a helo for this injury is a little bit of overkill, but anything with the head should be treated by a doctor."

"Will you—" Jesse started to shake his head, but trailed off to a soft moan and he reached for his head.

Cass spoke over Jesse's objection. "No, we don't need a helicopter for access unless you think this is a life-threatening situation. We're less than half mile from a BLM road."

"Let me—" With Bryan's help, Jesse pushed himself into a sitting position and rested his forearms on his bent knees. "This isn't any worse than falling off a bronc or getting mashed upside the arena wall. Trust me. If there's one thing I know, it's when I hurt enough to stay down. And this ain't even close."

Bryan blew out a breath. "Cass, I think he can make it to the road, if you want to have someone meet us there with a truck. I know he thinks he's the shit, but then again, all you cowboys have manure for brains, and he needs to go get checked out." Bryan smoothed a hand over the back of Jesse's head, and the big man winced.

"Okay, tell me what we're dealing with and I'll call it in."

"The biggest concern is concussion. Besides the wound on the side of his head, he's got one hell of a goose egg on the back. They're going to want to check for cranial bleeding. I don't see any indication of broken bones, he doesn't seem to be in extreme pain anywhere else. They'll want to clean the wound, check for any hidden injuries, and probably take a couple of x-rays. I imagine they might even keep him overnight for observation, but it looks to me like this old boy's got a big old banged up head."

"I ain't fucking old. Why does everyone seem determined to put me into retirement? Goddamn. I swear if I was a dog you all would have me put down. And that's another thing I've been meaning to talk to you about, Cartwright. Why the hell don't you have dogs on this ranch? If you had dogs, no one could have gotten into your yard without a shitload of barking. Then Chad's dorm would still be standing and he would have what he needs in order to make sure those kids coming out here have a good time. I have half a mind—"

Chad started laughing. "Okay show's over. I think this cowboy is going to make it."

"Maybe so, but that doesn't mean we're not getting him checked out. Can he walk far enough to get to the road, Bryan?"

"Let's help him to his feet and find out."

Ignoring the other man's outstretched hands Jesse pushed to his feet with only a small grunt of pain. "I don't need the hospital."

"Maybe not," Cass acknowledged. "But my insurance says that you do. You can start making your way due north. I'll bring up the rear and the horses after I call for Whit to bring the truck around. Chad? Will you be able to drive Jesse to Kingman?"

Chad looked up at Jesse, a silent request on the other man's face. Hoping he was interpreting the look correctly Chad nodded. "Yes, I can take him."

"Okay, you two start walking, Bryan and I will get the horses and catch up. Goddammit, Jesse, I am serious. If you start to feel like shit, sit down before you fall down."

As they walked over the uneven terrain, Chad wondered if he should wrap an arm around Jesse's waist, or if that would be insulting to his tough guy pride. He looped a finger through the back of Jesse's waistband just to keep his hands close. They walked in silence for a few minutes, Jesse staring at the ground and taking careful steps.

"What happened? Did you fall off Angel?" Chad asked after a minute.

Jesse started to shake his head, then stopped with a wince. "I don't know—I don't think so. I remember heading east. I was going to spend the morning riding that last little bit of fenceline I didn't get to the other day. I, uh...wanted some time to think... Then"—he frowned—"there was something..."

"It's okay, don't worry about it right now. I think short-term memory loss is sort of common after a head injury, right? I bet you'll remember soon enough."

Jesse stumbled slightly, and Chad wrapped his arm around Jesse's lean waist.

"Yeah, I suppose. I...uh...woke up and you were there. I don't know what happened. How did you know I was in trouble?"

"Angel showed up without you. He brought me back here."

"Angel? Wait...you rode Angel?" Jesse stopped and glared down at him. "Are you fucking nuts? That horse is way too big, too hard to control. You could have been killed. Didn't you learn—"

"Don't. Don't go there, Jesse. And you're welcome, by the way. I'm not exactly sure why, but I think Angel must like you, too. The damned horse brought me straight here—like some sort of equine St. Bernard."

The cowboy needed to keep calm and get to help as soon as possible, not fight and fuss at Chad. Besides, Jesse was right—Chad *was* an idiot for getting on a horse like Angel. That horse was as tall and as spirited as Rajun' had been when he was a child. The difference was, he was an adult now, and he'd believed the man he'd come to care about was in trouble. Yes, in retrospect, he could have been killed. That knowledge wouldn't have stopped him.

Chad grabbed Jesse's hand and pulled him forward. He could make out the flat ribbon of gravel road that cut through the chaparral landscape. They were almost there. After weaving their way through the last ten feet of scrub, they made the road and Chad forced Jesse to sit on the ground while they waited for the ranch truck. He could hear Cass and Bryan as they closed the distance.

Looking down into that strong, weathered face, covered with blood, dust, and dirt sticking to his wound, Chad realized the fright of seeing Angel come back alone, then finding an unconscious Jesse had resolved any lingering questions about his feelings. He no longer thought he was falling…he was already there. For whatever reason, this man was it for him. Not that he was going to say as much—at least not right now.

With a gentle finger, he traced the uninjured side of Jesse's face, noticed the slightly gray tinge to the normally tanned skin, the deep lines etched around the tight line of his mouth.

"What is it about you, Jesse Duran? First Angel, then me…you seem to have a way with the ranch misfits."

Chapter Twelve

The ride back from Kingman was long. Especially when neither of them were talking. Jesse couldn't think of one damn thing he wanted to say. Okay, there was plenty he wanted to say, he just couldn't figure out how. He was no good at real talk. Yeah, could talk his way into a stranger's pants, but now that it was important—he had nothing. Chad stared straight ahead, his hands at the ten and two, knuckles white, jaw working as if there was something on his mind, but Jesse had already told him he didn't want to talk about the doctor's news.

After the expected diagnosis of a concussion, the doctor had admitted Jesse overnight for observation and said she'd wanted to talk with him in the morning before she okayed his release. Damn, if Chad hadn't stayed with him all night, slumped in the fake leather recliner like they were partners or something. In fact, if Jesse hadn't asked Chad to leave when the doctor came in, there was little doubt he would have sat there through the final exam and conditional release. As it turned out, Jesse had been justifiably concerned with what the doctor would tell him, so asking Chad to step out had been the right decision. Letting him stay would have made it look like they had some sort of future, and Jesse couldn't let this thing between them go on. It wasn't fair, he knew that—but what the fuck in life was?

As they pulled into the yard, Chad coasted the truck to a stop directly in front of their casita, instead of the usual spot near the barn. Jesse opened the door, intent on finding Cass and making alternative sleeping arrangements.

"Come on, Jesse—in you go."

"I need to find Cass. Tell him what's going on…"

Chad leveled a look at him. "You need to tell me what's going on, too, so you might as well tell us both at the same time. Cass already texted me and is on his way over. Now, go inside."

Somehow that level teacher's stare had been a lot easier to withstand when Chad had been just another mountain to climb. Jesse needed to put the irritating man back in his appropriate box. Yeah, he was seriously thinking about settling down—there was no longer any choice in that matter—but he wasn't the man for Chad. There just wasn't room in his life for a relationship type of complication.

"Whatever. You all have your say, then I'll tell you the way it's going to be."

Chad's smile was easy, confident, and maybe just a little too understanding. "Jesse, take a deep breath. This is all going to work out. You go on and get settled on the couch and I'll bring our stuff inside."

Squinting across the yard, Jesse saw Cass step outside and head their way. There was to be no reprieve. With his hand on the door of the truck, Jesse carefully turned around and focused on getting to the front door without assistance. He was not about to admit to the wave of dizziness that washed over him the minute he stepped out of the truck.

Once he was inside the cool interior of Chad's casita, Jesse flopped onto the couch stretching his full length. He groaned and wished he'd removed his boots before he lay down, but he wasn't going to get up to remedy the situation. As much as he hated to admit it, the drive from Kingman had worn him out. With his head pounding and his eyes protesting the bright desert sunlight, all Jesse really wanted to do was nap. Covering his eyes with his arm to shield some of the light piercing his closed lids, Jesse decided to rest for a minute.

Coming slowly back to consciousness, Jesse was aware that he'd been sleeping, but unsure for how long. He dropped his arm and looked blearily around the room.

"Hey, Jesse, glad to see you home."

"Cass." He pushed himself upright and noticed his boots had been removed. Chad must've been making himself busy. "Sorry about dozing off, was I asleep long?"

"Not long enough," Chad said. "The bedroom is cool and dark, you can head in there as soon as you tell us what's going on. What did the doctor say?"

With a hand that shook more than he wanted it to, Jesse touched his temple, his fingers brushing against the gauze patch that covered the small wound. Jesse made a decision to come clean. Mostly. He didn't want their sympathy, but he needed a place to stay while he sorted his life, and the WSR was as good a place as any. But he also wasn't going to pussyfoot around the issue. He needed his own bunk—Chad was already unreasonably attached—and any pity would make it worse.

"I had a concussion. They wanted me to stay overnight for observation because the doctor didn't like some of the test results. She scheduled more tests for next week, but she also says competitive bronc riding is likely out of the question for the foreseeable future."

While Jesse had been talking, Chad down sat next to him on the couch. At his words, Chad reached over and squeezed his thigh, but didn't say anything.

Cass leaned forward and propped his elbows on his knees. "Foreseeable future. Uh huh. I'm going to go out on a limb here and say the doc told you the rodeo circuit is what you did and now it's time to find something else to do. She's retiring your ass."

Jesse grinned. "Busted. But I figure I have a couple of weeks for these tests, and by then, my brains will unscramble and I'll sweet talk her into signing my release. "

"So you expect to stay here until that happens?"

Jesse frowned. "I thought you were planning on me working here for another couple of weeks anyway. Is that going to be a problem?"

Cass stood, mashed his cowboy hat on his head and looked down at Jesse. "What are you? Thirty-six, thirty-seven?"

At Jesse's nod, Cass continued. "You and me...we're just about the same age. A year ago—I was content with the way my life was laid out. I was doing exactly what I wanted and I did it my own way. I didn't do relationships because I didn't want the drama. There's nothing like being your own man...it's the cowboy way, right?"

Jesse nodded, and even though he knew he was about to get hit head on, he couldn't look away.

"Then Ty walked into my life—bringing a boatload of trouble, right from the start. I swear to God, he had me breaking my own rules the first day I met him. Hell—before I even sat down to dinner."

"Point?" Jesse knew what the fucking point was, but goddamn if he was ready to acknowledge it. Besides, it wasn't the same damn thing at all. Chad was younger than Ty. He hadn't gotten a chance to really live.

Cass inhaled, as if he was going to continue, but Chad squeezed Jesse's leg once more then stood up and moved toward the door. "Thanks for stopping by, Cass. I think Jesse probably got your point. If not, then his brain is still too garbled to make the connection and it's not going to do any good for you to connect the dots for him.

"Let me walk you out." He nailed Jesse to the couch with a look. "Stay right there."

They stood in the doorway, where Jesse could both see and hear their conversation. "Cass, I've got until Monday before Alex returns and we're back to our school schedule. I know we need to talk about the Ranch Quest for the kids, but that's going to wait a day. Jesse and I are both taking tomorrow off. Don't call, don't come over, and tell Ty to keep his baked goods to himself."

The big rancher looked over Chad's shoulder, wearing what could only be called a shit-eating grin. With a quick wink, he turned and sauntered off, whistling softly through his teeth. Chris LeDoux's *Whatcha Gonna Do With a Cowboy*. Cute.

Then the door closed, and they were alone.

Chad turned to face him. "Come on, cowboy, let's get you to bed."

"I'm fine right here." Jesse felt foolish. He knew he sounded like a petulant child, but getting into Chad's bed right now was a bad idea.

"No, you're not." Chad's eyes narrowed. Without leaving any room for argument, Chad pulled him to his feet and practically dragged him to the bedroom and set him down on the edge of the bed.

"Hands up, lover." Chad pulled at the hem of Jesse's shirt and tugged it over his head.

"Not your lover."

"Shut up." Chad dropped to his knees and took one of Jesse's socks off, then the other, then rubbed his hands up the inseams of Jesse's jeans. His thumbs dug in hard, sending shockwaves of desire ricocheting through Jesse.

"Not right..." Jesse tried again.

Chad ignored his weak protest and began to work open the buttons on his jeans. Jesse watched as his own cock betrayed him by springing free from its confines as soon as Chad had the fly unfastened.

"Lift." Chad yanked the jeans down and left them in a pile on the floor as he pushed up to his feet.

Sitting there without a stitch on, he felt more than naked—he felt exposed soul deep. "Look, Chad—I appreciate what you're trying to do, really I do. I...uh...I'll ask Cass about another place—"

Chad shoved against his shoulders, knocking him flat on the mattress. "No. You lay right there. This time, I'm in charge and you can take what I dish out for a change."

****

Jesse's eyes went wide and Chad quickly pulled his shirt over his head to hide the laugh that threatened to escape. Well, cowboy, tough shit for you.

Tossing his shirt on the floor, Chad narrowed his eyes at Jesse, determined to have the truth. "Did the doctor restrict your activities? I mean in the bedroom..."

"No, but that's not gonna solve—"

"Good," Chad said, and pushed his own pants to the floor. "Scoot back."

As soon as Jesse moved, Chad dove for the bed, landing between the long legs spread open for him. Jesse let them drop open even wider, giving Chad some level of hope this wasn't going to be a fight. He climbed up to plant a kiss on the beautiful wide mouth. He could get lost in Jesse's kisses, just stay right there for a week and forget about his plan to make Jesse desperate for him. Lifting his head, Chad started to work his way down, beginning with Jesse's neck. Quick, hard nips, enough to leave marks if Jesse was foolish enough to try to go outside without his shirt on tomorrow. Jesse threw his head back and rested his hands lightly on Chad's shoulders.

With an open mouth, Chad ran wet kisses down Jesse's tanned chest, brushed his lips over the furred chest, and licked his way over the tight, lean abs. When Jesse's hips bucked and he pressed at Chad's shoulders with a husky moan, Chad knew exactly what the other man wanted. Instead of giving in, he moved back to Jesse's neck and started all over again.

"Fuck." Jesse's voice fit him like his favorite pair of jeans, soft and worn, and more than a little distressed.

Chad made the next trip much more slowly, pausing to lick and nibble at the tight copper nipples, to make hard stomach muscles jump under his tongue and teeth. He paused long enough to suck up a dark bruise on the pale flesh of Jesse's hip. His hips rolled, and Chad took mercy on the man and licked his way down the dark trail of hair below Jesse's navel.

"Yessss," Jesse hissed.

With one teasing kiss on the shaft of Jesse's hard cock, Chad ducked down to nuzzle at his balls and lick at the smooth skin that led to his hole. They'd never talked about who did what to whom, but given Jesse's open mouth, short breaths, and frequent gasps, he didn't think there was going to be any objections.

Jesse raised his hips and Chad scooped both cheeks into his palms and lifted that fine ass to his mouth. The first flick of Chad's tongue across the tight puckered hole brought Jesse's head up, his eyes fixed on Chad as if he wanted to see everything Chad was doing.

"Please…oh, God. Yes." Jesse flopped one leg over Chad's shoulder, a slight pressure, dragging Chad forward, still trying to drive the pace from the bottom. Chad flicked again and again, keeping the pressure light, teasing, tasting. As the tight muscle relaxed under the steady workout, Chad used his thumbs to hold Jesse open, tongue working deep until Jesse's thighs trembled and a harsh stream of curse words and pleas tore from a throat rubbed raw from need. Chad closed his eyes for a moment, savoring the intimacy. When he opened them again, Jesse's dark gaze was burning, intense.

Chad groaned and let Jesse's leg fall from his shoulder as he came to his knees and reached for the condom and lube on the nightstand. He gloved up, then jacked himself with a lube-slicked palm. Jesse watched every movement. He spilled more lube on his fingers, then spread Jesse's cheeks with the other hand while he inserted two fingers to test his readiness.

"Shit. Now." Jesse's voice was a sexy growl.

With the head of his dick pressed against Jesse's hole, Chad meant to take his time, to tease his way in, but his lover had other plans. Pulsing his hips upward, Jesse impaled himself on Chad. He lost control and slammed all the way in, but Jesse didn't seem to mind. He gripped Chad's hips with hard fingers, and moving together, they set a pounding rhythm. Jesse's legs and ass were tight, strong—and he used every muscle to make each stroke count. Squeezing, pulsing around Chad, rocking into each hard thrust.

Sweat soaked Chad's scalp, his hair was plastered to his forehead and cheeks. Drops of sweat trickled down his spine, tickled over his rib cage, as they slammed together, the slap of skin against skin, hips snapping. A long, hard ride. Just when Chad thought he couldn't last another minute, Jesse dropped one hand and brought it to his cock, the rough skin of his knuckles brushing against Chad's belly with the quick jerk of his fist.

With the first splash of warmth against his belly, Chad felt the last bit of his control slide away. He finished in a pounding assault on Jesse's spasming ass, until he was drained and sore.

He dropped on top of Jesse, not able to move even far enough to the side to roll off—just lay there, sucking in air, muscles quivering. "Just a second...I'll move."

Jesse shifted beneath him and thought he might be nodding.

When he was reasonably sure his heart would stay in his chest, Chad pushed off Jesse and sat back on his haunches. He smiled down.

"Damn, Jesse."

"No shit."

He removed the condom and tied it off. Not at all confident his legs would support him all the way to the bathroom and back, Chad just tossed it on the floor along with the wrapper. They weren't going anywhere.

"Now do you believe me?"

Jesse pushed up on his elbows and tilted his head to the side. "What are you talking about?"

"I'm talking about perfect. Destiny. Fate. Whatever you want to call us. You. Me. Together. You're not sleeping on the couch. You're not moving to a bunkhouse. You belong right here."

Jesse raked a hand through his hair. "God, Chad…I know, I'm not completely stupid. I swear I'm not. But you're not listening to me. You are too…"

"What? Too young? Are you still on that? In ten years, you're going to be forty-seven and I'll be thirty-five. You won't think anything about an age difference, then. You'll just be damn glad we spent the decade together, building a home together, and"—he paused for effect—"fucking like bunnies." This time when Jesse laughed the smile reached his eyes, and Chad continued.

"When we're together like this, there's no too short, too tall, no young or old, smart or brave or whatever. It's just us. You want to follow the rodeo? Then I guess I'll have to go with you. Because I'm not letting you go, Jesse. You mean something to me—and I know I mean something to you."

Jesse blew out a breath. "Come here," he said, and pulled at Chad's hands, dragging him down, so that their chests brushed together. His cowboy used hands rough as rawhide and gentle as a feather to brush the hair back from his face. "I've never thought of myself as a coward, but maybe I was as wrong about that as I've been about everything else."

Chad started to protest, but Jesse slid his fingers to Chad's lips, telling him without words to wait.

"I'm finished on the rodeo circuit. Even without the doctor's orders, it was time to hang up that dream. It's been a great ride, and I don't regret one minute of it, but now—" Jesse grinned up at him. "Warning, really corny cowboy talk ahead." When Chad nodded, Jesse continued. "For the first time I'm on a ride that means more than a buckle. I think...I'd like a home. *You* feel like home."

Smiling, Chad kissed the fingers that were pressed against his lips, then pulled back just far enough to speak around the tightness in his throat. "I'm going to make sure you stick this ride, cowboy."

~~The End~~

About the Author

Raised in California, Laura likes it hot, which explains why she ended up in Arizona via such diverse places as Japan, Maine, and Florida, and many more places in between. After retiring from the US Navy, she found a niche working for land management agencies, including the National Park Service and the Bureau of Land Management. Though she has held many jobs around the world, her favorite was working and living in Grand Canyon National Park. Working (and eating) in New Orleans was a close second. You will find many of her books are set against the rich backdrops provided by coastal Louisiana and northern Arizona.

When asked how she started writing, Laura tells of waking on Boxing Day a few years ago, with a woman named Elena MacFarland yammering in her dreams, demanding her story be told. Despite never attempting to write fiction before that morning, Laura ignored all of the holiday visitors and the Highland Destiny series was born. She doesn't believe it was a coincidence that the great grandmother who died when Laura was just a baby was named Elena MacFarland. Destiny does play a hand.

Laura became a full-time writer in 2012, and now she spends her time writing, watching her Arizona Diamondbacks, and working on her very own version of the Willow Springs Ranch in northwestern Arizona. She is a multi-published author of erotic romance, mystery, and urban fantasy and her books can be found at all major online retailers.

Connect with her online:
Twitter: http://twitter.com/lauraharner
Facebook: http://facebook.com/lauraharner
For her blog, book news, and to read free excerpts visit: http://lauraharner.com

Other Titles Now Available

Hot Corner Press and Pulp Friction Books

(Promotional material not included in word count.)

Willow Springs Ranch Boxed Set

This eVolume contains the first three books in the Willow Springs Ranch Series:

Ty Hard:

Tyler has used Don't Ask, Don't Tell as a shield against the truth since he was seventeen. Now, Ty finds himself cut loose from his Navy career after months of rehab from a debilitating head injury. At a loss as to what to do with his life, he travels to Willow Springs Ranch in Arizona to visit his surrogate father, only to arrive minutes after his oldest friend's death. Ty must come to terms with the loss while he fights to keep the PTSD from pulling him under. The last thing he's ready to think about is his growing attraction for another man.

Rancher Cass Cartwright's relationships never last more than a few hours, and that's just the way he likes it. Now he's in danger of doing the one thing he swore never to do: fall in love. Can Cass convince Ty to let go of his past or will sabotage at the ranch kill their love before it has a chance to grow?

Hold Tight:

Sheriff Holden Titus had organized his fresh start down to the last detail. Except for the part about the bomb that blew his plans all to hell. Now he's running out of time, without a job, without a home, and struggling to get back on his feet. Literally.

Despite the impolite rejection, Drew knows he didn't have the wrong impression months ago when he asked the sheriff to dance, but he never expected to have Holden's life in his hands. Literally.

Thanks to some meddlesome matchmaking, the two men are now temporary housemates at the Willow Springs Ranch and Drew is determined to help Holden heal, both physically and emotionally. Even if it means he has to drag the other man kicking and screaming to physical therapy...and out of the closet. In fact, that might be kind of fun.

The problem is, Holden doesn't consider himself in the closet...but not all secrets are created equal.

Taking Chance:

Officer Chance Carter is pretty sure he'd still enjoy being on either end of a good ass reaming-- just not the one from his supervisor that lands him on an involuntary extended vacation. Another holiday season with nothing to do except visit an old friend.

Former hospital corpsman Bryan Mitchell doesn't feel less than honorable, but that's what his discharge paperwork states. Now he is down and out in Kingman, Arizona until the charity of a stranger lands him a temporary job for the holidays.

When two federal employees go missing during a highly controversial wild horse roundup, the two Willow Springs Ranch newcomers are drafted to help in the search, but if rumors of a local anti-government militia are true, Chance and Bryan may be in serious trouble--and from something far more dangerous than their mutual attraction.

Chances Are by Lee Brazil

"I'm Chance, this is my place. You want me; this is where you can find me."

The problem with that, of course, was that it wasn't my name. My name was actually Aaron Dumont.

I picked up the name Chance as a kid when my grandma kept telling me "Chances are you'll come to no good, just like your pa." She had said it so often, it just kind of stuck. I've been Chance ever since. When she passed away and left me the remains of her estate, I sold everything but a few special items then invested it all in a nest egg for a rainy day.

I figured that's what she'd intended it for anyway. She'd said as soon as I joined the police force back in the eighties. "Chances are you'll come to no good there. It's a dangerous job and you're an accident waiting to happen."

She was right too.

Wicked Solutions by Havan Fellows

Sometimes the only way for justice to prevail is to get a little Wicked...

People who call him know the deal. He'll solve their problems, but he'll do it his way. That's the only way Wick Templeton plays the game. His years on the force and connections to all types of specialists put him in a league of his own. That's how he intends to keep it.

An ex-boyfriend in need puts Wick on a path that crosses that of Ned Harris, a stranger who proves to be a worthy adversary.

Wick's simple agenda gets a little more complicated. Item one: Clear his ex's name. Item two: unmask the enigma that is Ned Harris.

It's a good agenda. Too bad Wick can't seem to stick to it.

Triple Threat by Laura Harner

Master Archer found his forever with fellow Dom Zachary, but when their discreet recovery business interferes with their private time, Archer buys exactly what his lover needs—the perfect personal assistant, submissive Jeremiah. Because anything two can do, three can do better. Now the trio must work together to recover a grieving widow's stolen insurance money, and the thief is...her not-so-dead husband.

City Knight by T.A. Webb

What happens when two broken men collide?

Marcus works the streets of Atlanta, determined to keep it a safe place. An ex-cop, he buried his heart years ago. Ben works the same streets, selling himself to pay for college. The victim of a horrible crime, he decided to Just. Not. Care.

When their chance meeting leads to an unlikely attraction, will the ghosts that haunt them bring them closer, or separate them forever?

Caution: This is the first in a three part series, and you WILL want to come back for part 2. Hot men WILL have sex, and I can guarantee hot angst in my stories.

Second Chances Are by Lee Brazil

The ghost of his past keeps Aaron "Chance" Dumont from settling into his new relationship with Rory. Tired of coming in second place to a memory, Rory fights back in his own way with tragic results. Realizing that second chances in life are rare, Chance finally makes a decision...and then the past walks through his door.

Wicked Bindings by Havan Fellows

Wick Templeton is taken by surprise when a mysterious email is sent to his private address. Surprise won't stop him from hijacking an investigation of a serial killer. He's sure his investigative style won't mesh with the enigmatic Ned, but that's Ned's problem not his.

Together they will wear each other's nerves down, butt heads, raise libidos and maybe—if they are lucky, solve a few murders in the process.

Retribution by Laura Harner

When Dom Zachary walks out the door with Master Archer, leaving his inexperienced sub to wait for his attention, he never imagines the boy would call an abusive slave trainer with a grudge instead. Now they must find the missing Jeremiah and make the bastard who took him pay. Their salvage business has never been so personal.

www.ingramcontent.com/pod-product-compliance
Lightning Source LLC
Chambersburg PA
CBHW030257130626
46549CB00002B/572